DAY OF THE DEAD
A Romance

ERIK ORRANTIA

Dreamspinner Press

Published by
Dreamspinner Press
5032 Capital Circle SW
Ste 2, PMB# 279
Tallahassee, FL 32305-7886
USA
http://www.dreamspinnerpress.com/

Day of the Dead—A Romance

Cover Art by Catt Ford

ISBN: 978-1-62380-116-8

Printed in the United States of America
First Edition
November 2012

eBook edition available
eBook ISBN: 978-1-62380-117-5

For Jerry McCullough, a lifelong friend and a dedicated teacher, without whom many of the greatest turns in my life would have never happened… and very few of the bad ones.

ONE

THE buzz of the alarm clock infiltrated Joe's disturbing dream. He awoke and instantly forgot the dream, but its bitter taste lingered, mingling with his morning breath. He forced himself out of bed, the morning light from another gray summer day starting to appear between the blackness of the window frame and the pull-down blinds. Another day in foggy San Francisco. The Victorian floor creaked with every step. Every day it seemed more slanted. Or was he getting vertigo? He brushed his teeth at the leaky sink, fought with knotted shoelaces—Arturo had always told him to get slip-ons, but not with Joe's narrow feet—and headed down on foot from Noe Valley to the Mission. Cold gray sky matched the concrete sidewalk and something inside him, listless and melancholy.

Fifteen minutes later, he unlocked the restaurant door. He didn't even glance at the faded sign—"José Arturo Amor"—and hadn't noticed that the curl on the final *r* had worn off. Hell, he hardly noticed it was 2012 already. The light back in the kitchen meant Señora Darina, another illegal loyal to him through the years, had arrived. If only for Arturo's sake, Joe's commitment to protect her was undying. As he walked into the back, she flicked the switch on the mixer. "Good morning, Señor José," Joe read on her lips, the words accompanied by her smile of silver-lined teeth. He nodded back, mouthing, "Buenos días," and smiled as politely as he could. These days, living seemed like eating without taste buds. He chewed life and swallowed it because he had to.

He tied on an apron and pulled yesterday's salsas from the walk-in. A single roach crossed the floor in front of the stove. He crushed it with his black boot and curled his lip—a satisfying crunch. Time to call the fumigator. Yet another item on his list of things to do, a list that grew like black fungus on a wall in spite of Joe's halfhearted efforts to stave off its growth. He sighed out a heavy breath, a habit that had replaced so many exhales since Arturo had left him alone.

He glanced up at the wall clock. An hour before opening. Time had also become his enemy. It passed relentlessly slowly on those lonely, wakeful nights and then hustled when the world was upon him—lunch hour, the bills, the understaffed catering functions, the inspections. Was there some past misdeed he was atoning for? Had he sinned so wrongfully somehow that he deserved this agony? Was so-called God punishing him for something?

He sighed again and decided to start the chiles rellenos, assuming Chava would be late again. He brought a crate of poblano chiles to the stove. Just his luck—the chiles in this shipment were twisted and wrinkled, that much harder to properly roast. He set a bunch on the burners until they started crackling like cinders in a campfire, their acidic aroma rising up and penetrating his sinuses and bringing tears to his eyes, as they did every day. He hardly even noticed.

He heard a desperate rap on the door, but he did not respond with urgency. Chava's signature and chaotic style: every day he had a crisis, and some reason to be late, or in trouble. Joe left the chiles on the burner and went to the door. Arturo and Joe had always had sympathy for the kid. Besides, no one could make empanadas as tasty or tacos as quickly as Chava could. There was something about him that wouldn't allow Joe to let go of him, despite Chava's constant problems. Perhaps the simple memory of Arturo, as if he and Joe had been Chava's parents for all these years.

A red bandana covered the tattoos on the back of Chava's scalp. Who knew what weapon his baggy Dickies hid today, or from whom the weapon might be protecting him? He rapped again on the door, and Joe could see the dark green of the home-tattooed letters on his fingers, two joints up from his long, manicured fingernails. Chava was a fierce cholo, and yet the most effeminate queen, and he didn't take kindly to anyone who so much as tilted his head in judgment. He'd had more than his share of run-ins, and usually carried a butterfly knife that he'd brandish at anyone's glare. He called it his "eyes pick," and Joe thought it wouldn't be beyond him to gouge someone's meddling peepers right out of their sockets. If San Francisco weren't such a liberal town, where almost nobody batted an eye at others' differences, Chava would have been in jail for assault and battery long ago… or dead. Joe looked at the clock again. Chava had made it only fifteen minutes late this morning.

"What's up, boss?" Chava said with a smirk as he walked in. "Looks like somebody stomped on yo' face."

"Thanks. Put on your apron." Finally Joe let out a smile, or at least a frown, this morning, as if this wayward kid, or maybe this whole place, were still the reason, some reason, for him to keep on breathing. He'd let Chava take over the chiles and get on with the next most pressing task on the to-do list.

The day proceeded as every day did. Customers in, customers out. An occasional complaint, like no WiFi connection for customers' smartphones, the sound of a shattering dish, a homeless person asking for handouts, a crying baby, a drunk, and a compliment here and there. Joe went through the motions robotically, feigning interest in customers' suggestions and delight in their pleasure. As the lunch rush started taking shape, Joe tended tables to back up the wait staff.

"You ought to take a break, Joseph."

Joe looked up from his order pad at Alberto, his most regular customer. He disregarded the comment. "Will it be your usual, Alberto?" *Usual* meant a double portion. Alberto was so obese he hardly fit into the regular chairs anymore.

"Yeah. Let me try the enchiladas verdes today."

"Enchiladas verdes it is." He started heading back for the kitchen. This order would be given directly to Señora Darina. Ever since Alberto overheard Chava calling him *Al Puerco* the other day, the man didn't want Chava to handle his food. And Joe didn't exactly trust Chava, either, to make sure a hairy spider or rusty razorblade wouldn't end up on the big man's plate.

"Joseph," Alberto said in a deep, fatherly voice that made Joe stop and turn around. "I mean it. You need a break."

Joe nodded. It was probably true. But he had no one to cover for him at the restaurant, and though he could find no happiness here, there was no place he could think of that he'd rather be. The only person he wished to see was... well, he tried not to dwell on it.

Instead, he tried to occupy his mind during the downtime with mundane manual activities. Produce was ordered, meat stocked, schedules made. After the lunch rush, he stood himself in front of the chopping station to replenish the pico de gallo. What a ridiculous name, pico de gallo—cock's beak! What was that supposed to mean? Ever since he had learned Spanish—not the strict high school castellano version, but the Mission District brand—he had found humor in some translations that had never occurred to him before. Down in San Diego, for example, he had lived for a short spell near the Agua Hedionda Lagoon, in an upscale suburb of well-to-do gringos. Now he realized what nobody else seemed to know—they lived in "stinky water lagoon."

After dicing a bucket of tomatoes, he continued with cilantro and then onions. His hands worked autonomously as he focused on the walls they had enthusiastically painted five years before. His mind drifted to those glorious times. Fate had deceived him and retracted its blessing, as if he hadn't been grateful enough, as if he hadn't appreciated all that he'd had. Every memory brought him to an emotional ledge, a place where he could plunge into depression and sorrow. Tears began to well up in his eyes. Damned onions. He gave another slice. His finger cried out. Bright red on white. He dropped the knife on the cutting board and scrambled for a clean towel.

The physical pain jerked him back into the moment, superseding the emotional pain for now. He often wondered, though, because of the very real, painful sensation he often felt in his chest, if the nerve cells in his fingers weren't connected to his heart. As he applied pressure to the wound and surveyed the bloody mess, he forgot for a spell the nostalgic train he had been riding. But somewhere inside him, another energy had quietly been swelling, a concentration of hope and hurt stirring in anticipation of what had become an annual focus, a ritual, and a catharsis, only a couple months off now—the Day of the Dead.

TWO

AY, AMOR, what has happened to you? You only lament and drown in sadness.

I recall those pale cheeks of yours blushing with red the day we met. You hadn't brought any sunscreen. Nobody expected the October weather to be hot, yet the sun bore down on us all, packed shoulder to shoulder in the narrow streets. I never told you this, but I had spotted you from a block away. You were easy to see in the crowd—you were the tallest and whitest one there. We walked in opposite directions, and as you came through the swaying throngs, I made my way to your side of the street. I hadn't intended to bump into you so forcefully, or for the force of our collision to make us practically dance together right there in the street. But I'm glad we did. And I'm glad you had to go to the bathroom.

You probably thought that after thirty years of putting on the Festival Cervantino, the city would figure out how to provide public bathrooms, didn't you? Only a gringo would think like that, a gringo with the audacity to come to the Cervantino alone! You had hardly traveled through Mexico. Your Spanish was as bad as my English, yet someone back home put the spark in your mind and you ended up down the street from my porch.

"*Baño, baño?*" you said to me. Your eyes were desperate—you were about to explode. I knew it was drastic enough to take you to my emergency bathroom at a friend's grocery store. "WE DON'T LEND THE BATHROOM!" the sign said. It's good to have friends. In Guanajuato, we look forward to the Cervantino all year long. We prepare for it. Some families' businesses only open for that one week out of the whole year. Of course, the down side of all those visitors is that you have to wait for everything—a table in a restaurant, a bottle of water at the store, a space at the bar, and the bathroom.

You should see the town during other parts of the year—as dead as the exhumed bodies in the Mummy Museum. A charming dead, though, not a grotesque one. The narrow streets date back nearly five hundred years, some not even wide enough for cars. They make the perfect pathways for the Cervantino *estudiantinas*, the bands of young musicians in old-time clothes who parade through the town, their ukuleles attracting droves of followers who sing along to their nocturnal melodies. Without the bands, without the droves, the town is a place of romantic solitude.

We'd had an awkward moment when you stepped out of the bathroom. "Better?" I asked you. You nodded and wiped your brow in relief. "So…." Each man back on his original route? we wondered. Your blue eyes glimmered like star sapphires, your rosy cheeks like rubies, and I, the miner, had no thought of letting go of my quarry. "You want come with me?" I conjured from the English class files in my memory. You nodded as happily as you had after your bathroom relief. And I blew off my sister and her boyfriend for you. It was easy to say to them I got held up by the crowd.

I took you every place I could think of, and you followed along like a happy kindergartner. You responded to every six-word explanation I gave you as if it were the most profound seminar you'd ever heard. Every taco was a gourmet feast, every drink a satiating elixir. Even the *estudiantina* music filled your ears with utter delight, and you sang vociferously some interpretation of the lyrics you read off my lips. You were so silly, amor, and beautiful.

Late that night, or early the next morning, I should say, when the musicians finally tired and their group of followers dwindled, we decided to call it a night. "I'd better go look for a hotel," you said. You truly thought Guanajuato had enough hotel rooms for a couple hundred thousand people? Just walk on in and tell them you need a room? I told you there'd be no rooms—many people made reservations nearly a year in advance, and every hotel would have even put cots in their maintenance rooms and rented them at high prices. People were already asleep in the streets, on the sidewalks, in the park. Or was it your way of asking me for shelter?

The sofa had already been taken by my cousin's friend. Every bedroom was occupied. So you crashed on the floor of my bedroom. I tried to convince you to get up into my bed, but once you hit the floor you were dead asleep. I wedged a pillow under your head so your face didn't push against the tiles. We didn't get up the next day until after noon. I bet you woke up wondering where the heck you were. I remember everything, and now I see everything as if I were there again.

Do you remember the Callejón del Beso, our second awkward moment in as many days? People crowded in to the fabled place where the alley became narrower and narrower and the brightly painted homes on opposite sides became closer and closer together. Here the forbidden lovers came to their tragic end. Young Carlos spied Ana, his beautiful girlfriend, betrothed by her father to a rich Spaniard. When the man found out about Carlos, he forbade Ana to see him. So Carlos rented the home across the way, the two balconies within arm's reach. They would sneak nighttime visits and stretch across the way for kisses. But one night Ana's father, hidden in the shadows, caught them. He tromped upstairs to Ana's balcony and stabbed her in the chest in a fit of rage. Carlos jumped over to her from the opposite balcony and held her in his arms beneath the pale moonlight. Her silver tears fell as he kissed her lips one last time and said good-bye to his love forever.

Visitors now flock to the Alley of the Kiss, and couples stand beneath those opposing balconies. Photographers bid to catch the couples' kisses. Cameras flash, bystanders applaud, and then the next couple in line takes their place. We hadn't really meant to be in line. Your enthusiasm brought us closer and closer to the famous balconies as you angled your camera for snapshots. Before we knew it, we were in front of the line, and some photographer, the self-appointed coordinator, called up the next pair. Someone pushed us from behind, and before we knew it we stood beneath the balconies like the others had. An old man with an older camera brought it down for a second with a quizzical expression. "Oh... *jotos*," he said, eyebrows rising then falling again, and he brought the camera up to his face.

The crowd started chanting, "*Beso! Beso!*" as if it were a wedding. Hell, the cat was out of the bag. You looked at me with those sapphire eyes, your straight, white teeth glistening. I looked up at you, noticing again how tall you were. We shrugged and leaned toward each other for our very first kiss. Lights flashed from all around us, our tongues danced and twisted together, a cheer erupted, and you and I became inseparable from that instant, like Carlos and Ana, others' prohibitions notwithstanding.

We didn't get the photo. The old man's camera had run out of film. The next couple moved in, we pushed our way out of the alley, and we only kept the memory. Our first kiss, and our first little sadness too.

Another day exploring the city and watching the multitudes. Your amazement reminded me of how quaint Guanajuato was with its colonial buildings strewn about rolling hills, cobblestone streets, alleyways and staircases in irregular arrays. Plazas and taco carts stood on every corner, potted plants on second story balconies, women in aprons sweeping the street outside their homes until they stopped to gossip with the neighbors, and thriving old trees grew in strange directions on slanted embankments, roots clinging to bare rock. All those pictures you took. I had lived in Guanajuato almost my whole life and never had a photo of it.

Rain came down that second afternoon. Nobody cared, of course, and you and I got drenched in the street like everybody else. The musicians played under the awnings of restaurants closed for the night or beneath tarps haphazardly tied between light posts and tree trunks.

We made it back to my little house, soaked to the bone. We tried to keep quiet. My parents were asleep in the other room, my cousin's friend on the couch, and my sister, she probably stayed with her boyfriend. I peeled off your clothes in my bedroom, and you mine. We tried to contain our giggles as I shushed you. All I could think of was kissing you again. All day, I kept glancing at your lips, your pretty smile, and I wished to be in the Callejón del Beso again, where we could get away with it. Probably no one would have cared if we made out in the street, but not everyone knew about me and I didn't want them to see. That's why in my bedroom I practically attacked you—I couldn't stand the temptation anymore.

We made love intensely, and quietly. I didn't want my mamá to hear us. I didn't want her to find out. At least, most of me didn't. So we kissed like two lampreys feeding while we explored each other's bodies with our hands the same way we had explored Guanajuato—every valley, every hill, every opening. Your skin felt smooth on my fingers and palms, white like the sheets but silkier. And even much later I still fought myself to stave off my sleepiness because I wanted to stay awake while I was in your arms, pressed up naked against you. I wanted to feel you beside me, inside me all night long, and be inside you. And I wanted to possess you, claim you, and leave my marks all over your body. I didn't, of course. I couldn't blemish such a clean canvas. I couldn't own you. But I wanted to.

You stayed the next few days and met my parents and my sister. You were so polite to them. Every day you raved about my mother's cooking—you loved the beef soup and the chiles rellenos, even the smell of the roasting chiles in the air, and the spiciness of it all. You must have felt awkward when my mamá asked you about your girlfriend, and why you didn't have one, and didn't you want one? She knew, right? She must have known, but I still hadn't told her about myself and I can't blame her for wanting to carry on her delusion. And you seemed right at home, already starting to learn new Spanish words. "Idioms," you kept saying. "I have to learn the idioms." We all thought you were calling yourself an idiot, which seemed pretty harsh, but we were trying to also be polite to our new light-skinned guest from America. "Gabacho," my mother called you.

One of those days, I took you to see the Mummy Museum. We waited in line for hours, and we took advantage of the time to speak to each other, or learn to speak to each other. As you had taken Spanish in school so I had taken English, but nothing gets a lesson across better than motivation, and now I was motivated. Even when I had gone to the United States before, I didn't think much of English. I didn't care about it, and it seemed like such a flat language, technical, and impossible to read or spell. Wanting to know you and understand you made all the difference—I suddenly had a reason to finally learn the "th" sound and the difference between "ch" and "sh." Up until then, it had seemed like boring chit to me.

The mummies didn't impress you much. "They're not really mummies," you said. I hadn't realized you were like a scientist, too, reading every explanation, and then a language teacher, commenting on the poor translation. In Mexico, we don't always get the grammar right, but we have a certain affinity for goriness. The museum had the exhumed bodies displayed in cases in their naked splendor. Their hair had grown after death, even their pubes, and their yellow teeth stuck out against their brown, leathery skin. Infants with empty eye sockets sat upright beside a pregnant woman whose excess abdominal skin sagged like an old burlap sack. No, they weren't the kind of mummies the ancients had wrapped and purposely preserved. Something in the soil at the neighboring cemetery kept their bodies intact. People didn't go to see them for a history lesson—it wasn't King Tut displayed in a museum. They went because of a fascination with morbidity, the wonder of death, its finality, so close and yet seemingly distant.

There they were, yet they had died long ago. Dead like me. I'm not in a better place, or even a different place. I'm right here in the same place—with you in Guanajuato, with you in San Francisco—inside you and all around, like the first night in bed together, and every night after that. I'm in every place all at once, and in every moment. If only you knew.

THREE

"THEY have a fantastic two-in-one menu." Joe put on a patient face as Sarah, a longtime customer, explained the menu to her friend. She flipped it over and pointed to pictures that Joe noticed were faded. The laminate on the menu had bubbled and cracked, not unlike the Formica on the tabletop. "You can get a torta and a taco or a burrito and a tostada, see? They have all sorts of choices… and they're all good, right, Joe?"

"If you say so, Sarah."

Two-in-one. Arturo's idea. Joe had assumed they'd offer combination plates like any other Mexican restaurant. Arturo, ever the romantic, had insisted they called them *two-in-one.* "It's like us," he had said. "We're two-in-one, amor. José and Arturo forever. We're different—you're the white flour tortilla, I'm the mole, but we're two together on one plate."

"You're cheesy."

"Cheesy mole? You don't put cheese on mole, amor."

"It's an expression."

"Like my sad face without the Two-in-One."

And thus the restaurant had been established. From the name to the color of the chairs and walls, the recipes, the dishes, the uniforms of the workers, and the arrangement of the bar, everything was negotiated with what Arturo called Joe's "logical gringo thinking" and Arturo's spontaneous creativity. The place and everything inside it belonged to the two of them.

Officially, Arturo did not exist, a fact that had never settled well with Joe. Though they knew the place belonged to both of them, there was no way to put Arturo's name on the license, or on the lease, without exposing him as an illegal. Joe's partner could have no car or property or Social Security number. Even registering with the state as domestic partners could have been a risk, not to mention the constant possibility of an INS raid on the restaurant. Lucky thing San Francisco was such a liberal city, but even so, in any sudden Immigration push, the Mission District would be an obvious target.

"It doesn't matter, amor," Arturo had said. "It's your money, anyways. Your retirement."

"It does matter, though," Joe answered. "If you were a woman, we'd be married and you'd have papers by now."

"If I were a woman, then you would have to be straight and lick my twat."

"Don't be gross."

"Don't worry about the paperwork. I know this place is ours because I have faith in you. Anyway, you can be upset, but there's nothing we can do about it."

"Doesn't it make you mad? Where's that Latin fire?"

Arturo shrugged. "I could be mad. But I don't want to. Where I come from, we don't worry about the papers like you do. It's all just a game. Look, we have a restaurant, don't we? I don't need my name on the paper when I have ladles and spatulas in my hand."

Just as well, Joe realized. It might have been pretty complicated now if he'd had the name of a missing person as his business partner. Then again, if things were fair, Arturo wouldn't have had to trek through the desert mountains to come home to his partner, would he? He would have crossed the border like any other dignified, married straight person.

Missing person. The police wouldn't even make a report on a person who disappeared somewhere between Tecate and San Francisco. "I'll be there in two or three days. I love you." Arturo's last words. Actually, he'd said "two or *tree* days"—he still hadn't gotten the *th* sound quite right. Joe waited a week before he really began to worry.

After ten days, he went down to Southern California and drove the stretch of Interstate 8 along the border, as if he'd find Arturo sitting on the shoulder. He went to every law enforcement agency he could think of and, finally, to the Customs and Border Protection detention center.

"Arturo García López," Joe pronounced through a metal screen to the officer behind the bulletproof window.

"I got no one by that name in the last two weeks, sir. But they usually don't give us their real names."

"I think he may be missing. Something might have happened to him."

"Well, sir, our job is not to go out looking for him so we can bring him to you. In fact, these people are generally trying *not* to be found by us."

"He could be dead."

The blank-faced officer nodded. "It happens."

"So what am I supposed to do?"

"I don't recommend looking for him. Most of the border terrain is restricted area and all of it is hazardous. They don't understand how dangerous it is. Besides the weather, they get lost, and there are plenty of bandits out there, and other snakes too."

"How will I know if you find him? Do they get a phone call?"

The officer shook his head. "You wouldn't have a copy of his fingerprints, would you?"

"No."

"For all I know, your friend's been processed and deported already. He'll probably call you. And I advise you to discourage him from attempting to cross again. You could be getting yourself in trouble, too, for aiding and harboring an illegal."

"What do you mean?"

"It's a federal crime to assist in the illegal transfer of—"

"Okay, I get it. Do you want to arrest me for worrying about my partner, who may be dying in the mountains? Go ahead." He turned around and walked out of the office.

A day or two later Joe returned to San Francisco, after having left Chava and Señora Darina in charge. At first he had hoped to find Arturo somehow, and then he hoped Arturo would be miraculously behind the counter at the restaurant upon his return. Arturo never showed up. So he spoke with Arturo's mother in Guanajuato, after having resisted calling her in her delicate state—he hadn't wanted to worry her. As he suspected, she knew as little as he did. Arturo had left, she told Joe, determined to make it back "home" after having his tourist visa denied. He wouldn't be kept away. She had prayed for him, and said the rosary, for all the good the prayers would do, and now both of them worried. She'd had some serious health concerns, the reason for Arturo's return to Guanajuato in the first place, and this would do her no good.

"Okay. Two two-in-ones. Hers with the giant shredded beef enchilada and the *sope*, and mine with a chimichanga and the chicken thingy I like—what's it called?" Sarah snapped Joe out of his hypnosis.

He shook himself awake. "Umm… it's a quesadilla."

"Yeah, right. A chicken quesadilla."

He jotted her order down.

"And a pitcher of those margaritas… strawberry."

"Got it." Strawberry margaritas, one of Arturo's favorites. Was there anything that wouldn't remind Joe of Arturo?

He clipped the ticket to the order wheel and spun it to the substitute cook. Chava hadn't shown again that morning.

Salvador was Chava's real name, Chava being the common Mexican nickname for Salvadors, and a somewhat cruel twist of fate for all of the childhood torment it brought on—*chava* also meant girl. His mother couldn't have known when he was born, could she?

Before the grand opening of the restaurant, he had come in for an interview in baggy pants and a long-sleeved shirt with only the top button fastened, and a new white A-shirt showing underneath. Joe's first thought—no way. But Arturo squeezed Joe's thigh under the table so he'd give the kid a chance. The kid hardly looked either of them in the eye, focusing on his tattooed finger as it scribbled imaginary graffiti on the table. And when he opened his mouth to speak, a tender, humble voice came out of the little thug's mouth. The seventeen-year-old constantly licked his lips, giving them a glossy appearance, and he explained without being asked how he had left his family in Gilroy, where his mother worked in a garlic-processing plant.

He went on to say that his two brothers were in jail, his sister was in her second pregnancy, his dad was a drunk, and he had been frequently harassed for being gay in high school, where he had been a junior. Finally, after suffering some problem for which the cops were probably after him, he had decided it was time to split. "Your parents let you leave?"

"My pops don't care and my Amá, well, she don't know what to do with me. I mean, she love me, but she can't do nothing for me. She don't really speak English, you know, and besides, she's mostly at the garlic plant. She gave me, like, fifty bucks and, like, ten kisses and crossed me. I decided to come here to San Francisco where people don't fuck with me... I mean, you know, mess with me... sorry about that... for being homo. So do you think you could give me a chance at something? I need to work 'cause I got to pay my friend some rent."

He told them his cell phone was busted so they asked him to come back the next day. Joe and Arturo had talked it over that night and made a decision.

"It's not really our place to tell you what to do, Salvador," Arturo said.

"Chava. Everyone calls me Chava."

"Okay, Chava. Look, we're just starting off this restaurant, and you're not exactly what we had in mind. But we've decided we're going to give you a chance because we need a dishwasher."

"I can wash yo' dishes."

"Okay. Good. We have a condition, though."

"What?"

"We want you to go to school," Joe said. "You should at least get your GED."

The kid first furled his forehead but then agreed, and he started the next day. Once Arturo discovered his aptitude for cooking, he taught him the recipes, and he became Arturo's kitchen assistant. Now twenty-two, with Arturo's absence, Chava had become the head cook. He had earned his GED, as promised. Unfortunately, he hadn't ridded himself of his ghetto side—he knew no other style of dress, his instinctive solution to conflict was aggression, and he was terribly unpunctual. Additionally, he was hypersensitive to judgment. At least he respected Joe and Arturo enough to listen to them. In any case, despite all his faults, Chava had become part of them, and they knew they were the only sort of decent family he had.

Joe had considered letting him go on several occasions. Now, especially after Arturo's disappearance three years before, he simply wouldn't do it. He had seen the kid grow up and knew he had talent, and Joe cared for him. He couldn't imagine Chava would make it any other place, nor could he imagine running the restaurant without him. He only hoped Chava would wake up and overcome his demons.

FOUR

AFTER we met, you and I were both more than happy to ignore the fact that you'd be leaving Guanajuato pretty soon. You had your job to return to, checking software programs for security flaws. I had heard about people who had vacation romances—a one-week fling to get the real foreign flavor and then good-bye forever. This felt different—since our dance in the crowded street, we had been inseparable.

I noticed you at times, the way you seemed to drift off in your thoughts between our conversations. I had no idea you were making plans, working out a scheme in your mind. I assumed you'd leave me, and maybe we'd chat online, or visit again in some unknown future. A day before your flight home, you held my hand and looked into my eyes. "Come with me," you said.

"Okay," I answered without another thought, as if I didn't want to give you a single second to take it back, or change your mind, or tell me you were only kidding. After I agreed, I thought for a moment. "And what will I do?" I sure didn't want to be a laborer again, working for less than minimum wage for people who figured they were doing me a favor so I had better do whatever they said.

"It doesn't matter. We'll figure something out, trust me."

I only had a year left on my tourist visa. Ten years pass quickly. So I figured there might not be another chance. I wasn't doing any serious work in Guanajuato. My family would miss me, just like the first time I went to the US, and I would miss them. A person has to give life a chance, right?

You got me a plane ticket over the phone and wouldn't tell me how much you spent on it. You were right—it didn't matter—because I didn't have any money with which to pay you back. I packed a duffel bag full of clothes, and then you came with me to the basilica in the center of town.

I saw your frown when I dipped my hand into the holy water and crossed myself. You always thought the religious traditions were ridiculous, but you sat patiently as I knelt in a pew and prayed before Jesús, beneath the high arches of the buttressed walls. You'd later mock my prayers.

Ay, amor, even then I knew it wasn't a private line to a man named God. You suggested once I write him a text message. For me, my prayers helped to focus my energy and manage the emotions swirling inside—fear, anxiety, blind excitement, and hope. I was meditating in a place constructed for it. Now I wish you'd be able to do the same and stir those feelings that have settled like sediment after a storm, first in waiting, now in dull mourning. Amor, there's a reason for prayer—it's not a mindless ritual of ignorant sheep. You're so much closer to your own salvation than you would ever believe, yet for now you've decided to wallow in misery and the lingering denial of what you know inside is true. Peace awaits despite your guilty feelings, but there's no need for forgiveness when there is no wrongdoing. You'll find out in due time, but for your sake I wish you would rise above your sorrow. I am not going anywhere because I am everywhere now. I won't be leaving you even when you decide to move on from me.

"Mamá, Papá, I'm leaving with Joe."

"You're going with José?" she asked. She'd already started calling you that because she'd said she felt like she was talking about herself, *yo*, when she said your name, *Joe*. "You hardly even know him. What do you think you will do up there? You hated living in Phoenix, don't you remember?"

I knew Mamá would worry. After all, she was right about all those things. I had just met you, I had no idea what I would do in San Francisco, and I had hated my eight-month stint in Phoenix. "Mamá, don't worry. I can always come back. And my visa's expiring. I might not be able to go afterward."

"Ay, my son." She raised her hands in prayer and looked up to the ceiling as if God were upstairs. "Take care of my son," she begged, nearly starting to cry.

"Mamá, don't get hysterical. This is an opportunity. Can't you see? And really I'll be only a stone's throw away."

"I'm too old to throw stones, Arturo." And then she turned to you, as if you were an adversary. "You." She shook her finger at you. "You better take care of my son, José."

"Yes," you said, nodding, "no need to worry, señora." You held your hands out in front of her and said in Spanish, "Good hands."

She insisted we all hold hands right there in the living room of our humble house. She grabbed those good hands of yours, pulled my papá and me into a circle, and prayed. Then, as if nothing had happened, she went straight to the kitchen and started preparing our going-away feast. We had planned on spending our last night together out in the Festival Cervantino, but we couldn't refuse Mamá her last meal.

"I'm going to miss your cooking, Mamá," I said over dinner.

She waved her hand. "No, son, you know how to cook everything I make at least as well as I do."

"I learned from the best."

"Yes, you did. I could never get you out of the kitchen when you were little. Now you could start your own restaurant."

I'd gobbled up those last morsels of motherly love and hadn't even noticed that she, like a gardener, had just planted a seed. If there were a God, then mothers would be his most precious gift.

Our trip to the airport turned out to be quite hectic. All those people in and out for the festivities. It took us an hour to get a taxi to take us to the airport twenty miles away, and another two hours to get there. There had been no time for nostalgia or sentimentality, just traffic and clock-watching, people and lines. I hadn't known I wouldn't be back for years, and I refused to imagine the circumstances that might cause me to return.

By nightfall we were in the bedroom of your second-floor Victorian flat. I had heard a lot about San Francisco and couldn't wait to see the Golden Gate Bridge, Alcatraz, and that super windy road. That night I was still legal. I had six months to be there as a tourist, and I figured it would take at least that long for me to get to know the city. But there'd be plenty of time to see the sights. That night we were weary and hungry. I looked inside your refrigerator and remembered one of the things I hated so much about Phoenix—I couldn't get a decent tortilla.

We had chow fun instead, from a Chinese take-out box like the kind I had seen on TV. Those boxes always made the food look more appetizing. "Fun?" I asked. "Like this is fun to eat? Chewy noodles and slippery onions?"

"No, it's a Chinese word," you said.

I was having enough trouble with English, and you expected me to start learning Chinese.

After dinner we went to bed. You held me close but we didn't make love. I heard the dripping faucet, the cars driving by, an occasional siren. I felt tired, but my eyes wouldn't close, so I looked at the walls and the strange shapes of things on your dresser. I tasted onions on my breath. You started to snore, louder than you ever had in Guanajuato, and it made me wonder if the air was different here, or if all the liquor we drank at the festival had dulled your snoring, or maybe my listening. I thought of Mamá and the pregnant mummy. I thought of our first kiss in the alley and the subsequent applause. I thought of Phoenix and the two-bedroom apartment I had shared with three other aliens like me. I hated playing straight with them, and I hated the thin sheetrock walls through which I could hear Rafael have sex with either of his American girlfriends. Returning home to Guanajuato from Phoenix had felt glorious, and yet there I was in the United States again. I wondered what I had done.

FIVE

CHAVA showed up at nine o'clock the next morning with his bandana stretched down near his eye and gauze taped on the length of his forearm. He avoided Joe's glare by putting his hands in his pockets and staring down at the floor.

"My God, what has happened to you?"

"Nothin'. I'm just going to the kitchen now, alright?"

"No. Chava, sit down. You've got to tell me what happened."

"Same shit, man."

Joe grabbed him by his good elbow to pull him toward a booth in the corner, but Chava yanked his arm away. "Don't touch me, alright?"

"Take it easy, Chava. You're with friends."

"Yeah, whatever."

"Either sit down or leave, Chava. I can't let you work like this."

Chava looked over at the door, Joe half supposing he would split. He noticed a swollen gash at the corner of Chava's eye, partly covered by the bandana.

"I'm trying to help you, Chava. You're lucky enough I don't fire you."

"Well, fire me, then!" the kid shouted in his high-pitched voice. "You may as well. Everyone else has gotten rid of me, one way or another."

"Come on, Chava. You know me better than that. Let's both take it easy and sit down for a minute."

Chava reluctantly stepped with him over to the corner booth, the one that Joe often used for personnel matters, and put his face down on his arm.

"What happened to you? Was it your roommate? I think it's time to call the cops."

"Are you stupid or something? It wasn't Dario and no one's calling no cops," he said, his face buried in the crack of his elbow.

"Let me see your eye."

Like a teenager wanting parental care yet resisting it, Chava pulled up the bandana enough to expose the wound. Joe winced. "What happened? Did someone cut you?"

"No. He hit me. Brass knuckles, I think."

"It wasn't Dario… so who was it?"

"I don't know, some dude in the street. I called his girlfriend a stank whore."

"Why?"

"Because she was one…."

"So? Why would you say that?"

"I was pissed off, okay? I think he said some shit to me. And then I had to find someplace to sleep, so I went over to Dolores Park."

An aptly named place, Joe later thought, and another ironic Spanish translation—*dolores* meant a type of flower and was also the plural of pain.

"Why didn't you go home?"

"I got in a fight with Dario. Fucker thought I'd be his bitch and I ain't nobody's bitch. He said I had two choices: pay the rent or give it up. I ain't the whore. That bitch in the street, she was a whore."

"You could have come to my house."

"I don't need no homeless shelter."

"What happened to your rent, anyway?"

"I don't know. I spent it. Had to pay something I owed."

"And your arm?"

Chava lifted up his head and looked at the gauze. "Motherfucker threw me down on the street like some kinda wrestling move." He laughed for a second at himself. "Big motherfucker."

"You got to stop picking fights."

"I know. I told you I was pissed."

"Well, can you work?"

"Yes, I can work. Why do you think I came here?"

"And you'll come to my house tonight?"

"Hey, I'll go to your house, but I told you I ain't no bitch. I ain't givin' it up for you, either."

Joe rubbed his face with both hands. "You're kidding, right?"

Chava looked at him with a childlike expression, eyes on the verge of gushing behind long, black eyelashes.

"Cover your eye with clean gauze from the first-aid kit and get to work, then."

"Alright. Sorry I didn't come in yesterday."

"You've got to learn to be more responsible."

"I know. I will."

Joe started to get up from the booth.

"Oh, um…." Chava said.

"Yes?"

"It's just… well… I just hope Dario won't come in here looking for me. I, umm, broke his TV on the way out… knocked it off the table."

"If he does anything, I am calling the cops."

"Oh, well, I don't think he will. Just thought it was fair to say something."

"I'll keep my eyes open."

"I won't—can't keep this eye open." He pointed up to his eye with his bandaged arm.

"Get to work, Chava. Keep cool."

Chava certainly had his problems, and now he'd be coming to stay with Joe. At least this way Joe could keep a better eye on him, and hopefully make sure he stayed out of trouble. After all, Chava wasn't the only one with problems. Everyone had defects, even Arturo. Joe leaned up on the bar, noticing the slender blue bottle of Corralejo tequila, Arturo's favorite brand. Sure, they'd had lots of drinks the first week they met, but that was the Cervantino in Guanajuato. Joe hadn't imagined that Arturo's drinking would spill over into the rest of the year. Of course, they had barely met, how could he have known? He had wondered later if Arturo had simply been on good behavior, or if Joe had ignored obvious signs of trouble.

Shortly after their arrival to San Francisco, when Joe had returned to the routine of everyday life at the software firm, Arturo spent his days tending their shared nest. As if marking his territory, he took the liberty of making adjustments to Joe's place. He hung a gaudy *sarape* on the dining room wall and found in the Mission everything he needed to put together a makeshift Catholic shrine, including a bloody, plastic Jesús crucified on a cross of sticks and a monthlong supply of *veladoras*, unscented candles in tall glass vases, each adorned with some gothic depiction of María.

He would also bring home small plastic bags of whole dried chiles, ground chile, *epazote*, and cumin, sacks of beans and rice, and anything fresh from the butcher, with which he'd put together the evening's meal. Cocktail hour would start around that time in the afternoon, while he worked in the house alone, lonely, waiting for Joe to come home.

"Amor, amor," he'd say as Joe would walk in the door, and Arturo would take his coat, just before the welcome-home kiss, in an act Joe construed at times as Arturo's way of earning his keep. He'd have liquor on his breath, having drunk three or four shots by the time Joe arrived. They'd been buying the biggest bottles of tequila they could find. The liquor at first would bring out Arturo's even more affectionate, playful side, and before bedtime, Joe would have drunk his share of margaritas as well. The second phase of Arturo's drunken state normally included a quiet, tearful spell, before he'd finally go to sleep, only to start the same routine the next day. His behavior was certainly tolerable—Joe could understand Arturo's need to spice up his day, especially being so far from kith and kin—but the sheer quantity of tequila his new partner could drink astounded him. Clearly, something would have to change or else an unrestrained vice would teeter into an insurmountable obstacle.

That era didn't last long, however. When Joe left for work in the morning, Arturo began getting to know the city, spending most of his time around the Mission District, practically a little Central America. He met people from up and down the Spanish-speaking world—Perú, Argentina, Honduras, El Salvador—though the majority were Mexican. Discussion about "papers" was commonplace, and almost everyone had a job of one kind or another, a fact that made Arturo feel like a bum. He'd talk about it with Joe, asking what he was going to do with himself. He had no interest in living off Joe for the rest of his life, or in being seen as the housewife. Though their relationship was growing and they spent long evenings together listening to Mexican music and watching English sitcoms that Joe translated, Arturo jumped at the first job offer he got.

He became a prep cook for a restaurant-cantina on the corner of Valencia and 17th Street—the dinner shift. Joe put up a little resistance, concerned about Arturo getting caught by Immigration—La Migra—and that the difference in their schedules would give them no time together. "Nobody over there has papers. They're all ready to dart out the door," Arturo answered eagerly. "And besides, it will only be for a while, until I find something better."

Seeing the enthusiasm in Arturo's eyes, Joe could hardly oppose the plan. He could imagine the monotony of moving to another country and having to stick around the house all day. They certainly hadn't thought their entire plan through. Still, Joe had no regrets, and despite the job and the tequila, he loved having Arturo in his life.

Eventually, Joe adjusted to heating up food Arturo would leave in the refrigerator, and to spending the evenings mostly alone. He almost felt single again, though he knew Arturo was there, at least, and that this arrangement was only temporary. Once in a while, he would visit the cantina and eat dinner there, but Arturo worked back in the kitchen and was kept busy. So usually Joe simply stayed home and went to bed by eleven, while one ear waited for the noise of Arturo coming home, quietly brushing his teeth, and then crawling into bed with Joe.

One night, about a month after Arturo had started the job, he didn't come home at midnight as usual. Joe awakened, realizing there'd been no key in the door, no footsteps up the wooden stairs, and no creak of the bathroom floor. He figured Arturo had stayed at work late, maybe a private party or something for which they needed him extra hours. A phone call would have been nice. He wrestled with himself to relax and go back to sleep. After all, he had to get up for work in the morning. The clock's ticking seemed to get louder, and the eeriness of silence became too much to bear. His wondering eyes were stuck open, and he finally sat up in bed. Two thirty in the morning. What if La Migra raided the restaurant? Or what if he'd been mugged? What if he went off with another… no, that was stupid. Arturo could be lying in the gutter someplace or sitting in a jail cell. And he had no ID with their address, nothing linking him to Joe. Joe wasn't even sure if Arturo actually knew the street address. He called the cantina—no answer. He thought about getting up and walking over there. It wasn't so far away.

He pulled on some jeans and a T-shirt and scrounged in the closet for a baseball cap. He hustled down the hallway and stairs. As he opened the door, he saw some people coming up the stairs outside toward the door. Could be the neighbors. Their speech was slurred and boisterous. Then he realized one of them was Arturo, clinging to the shoulder of a guy on either side of him. "Come on, amigo," one said, "just a few more steps."

"Are you José?" the other asked.

Joe nodded.

"We have a package for you," the first one said, laughing.

In unison, they pried Arturo's arms off their shoulders and landed them on Joe's.

"Said he could out-drink us, but now we see who's the king of the queens." The two chuckled as they turned and left. "See you tomorrow, 'Turo," one of them said before they disappeared down the block.

It took Joe ten minutes to get Arturo up the stairs, out of his clothes, and into bed. "What happened? Where'd you go? Who were they?" Arturo was totally out of it—he answered in incomprehensible blurts. A few minutes later, he was fast asleep. Joe remained wide awake and was only slightly consoled when Arturo nudged up against him in an instinctual embrace.

Late the next night, he explained to Joe that he had gone out with a couple Mexican guys from work, Chuy and Chepa, and he didn't understand what the problem was.

"You came home plastered, and didn't even let me know!"

"I did? Didn't I call you?"

"No."

"Oh, sorry. I meant to call. I... can't remember."

A flurry of apologies followed, and promises to not repeat the situation. Of course he should let Joe know if he was going out, he agreed. He had been excited to meet other gay guys from his state. He was glad they worked with him. They were really cool, and insisted he go out with them. The rest was a faded memory. It wouldn't happen again, he repeated and apologized, just as he did the next ten or fifteen times he did it.

No one was perfect, Joe knew. Everyone had defects. *Arturo drinks*, he thought, *but he still contributes a good portion of his paycheck, and he still takes care of his side of the relationship, when he's not drunk.* And wasn't it part of the Mexican culture, anyway, like the brightly colored serape in the dining room? Joe tried to view the situation simply as a clash of cultures. Arturo was entitled to a life, Joe reasoned, and he wasn't about to go acting like Arturo's parent. And aside from those incidents a couple times a month, Arturo was everything Joe had ever hoped for in a partner. He wasn't about to break up over it... not yet. The incidents piled up as months turned into years, during which time Joe maintained what he had said: "Arturo, one of these days, the bottle's going to kill you."

Joe was now thinking about the *ofrenda* for Arturo.

Arturo had disappeared in October, three years ago. At the time, the Day of the Dead was approaching, and Joe remembered the *ofrenda* Arturo always set up in the house for his grandparents. He had no photo of them, so on the little hallway table, on top of the serape he pulled down to use as a tablecloth, he placed a poem about grandparents he had found. Beside it, he put dishes of olives stuffed with jalapeños, his grandmother's favorite, and round sweet breads, *conchas*, for his grandfather. Then, on the second of November, he'd light a candle, arrange fresh flowers in a vase, kneel in prayer, and then play their favorite music all day.

The first October, when Arturo did not return, Joe had worried about the *ofrenda* for Arturo's grandparents. He waited, hoping Arturo would be back in time to set it up. Finally, on Halloween, he decided to make the *ofrenda* himself, imagining Arturo's pleasure when he came home to see it. A thought occurred to Joe then, which made him feel queasy—should he be making the *ofrenda* for Arturo? *Of course not,* he reasoned. *Let's not jump to irrational conclusions or let our paranoid imaginations run away with us. He'll be back,* he reassured himself, his eyes darting to the phone as had become his constant habit.

The second year, Joe made the *ofrenda* for Arturo. His fear of regretting not making it overtook his lingering denial. Now the third year, and only September, but Joe was already planning for it. He remembered those drunken nights, and the anger he felt at times with Arturo. Now he'd give anything to hold him in his arms again, drunk as a skunk, slurring and slobbering like an idiot. Joe would be more than happy to serve up the next round of shots. Standing in front of the bar at the restaurant, he would sometimes look at the bottle of Corralejo, never quite able to figure out why they'd put tequila in such an oddly shaped container. The blue bottle measured nearly two feet tall and made pouring hard for even a sober person. It was Arturo's favorite— Joe would include the bottle this year in Arturo's *ofrenda*.

SIX

YOU were right about the bottle killing me.

I grew up around the bottle. On a normal day, my papá would have at least a couple beers and a few measures of tequila. If my uncles came by, as they often did, then a reason for drinking materialized. Mamá didn't complain much about it, because she liked that her husband got along with her siblings, and once in a while she'd join in too. My papá was always a tranquil man, even while he drank, and when his health reports started getting worse, he laid off the bottle a bit.

My sister was always the rowdy one. She had dropped out of school and let her boyfriend support her, so she figured that until she got married and pregnant she might as well live it up, and her life was a year-round Cervantino. She'd been brought home by the police a few times—good thing some of them were grade-school friends of my papá—for unruly behavior in a downtown bar, the one she and her boyfriend most frequented, three doors down from the basilica. My parents never said much about it because they had been young once too, and I always got a good laugh from her stories about dancing on the tables or rolling on the floor. Not a big deal.

You, on the other hand, worried about everything—was the house locked, were the bills paid, and was everything in its little place? You talked a lot about money and retirement and some 401 account. I thought with all the money you put in it the number would get bigger, but you always said, "We're not touching the 401(k)." I couldn't imagine what was so special about $401,000, but it seemed like enough money for us to live on forever. Back home it would have been.

You also worried about my drinking. I never thought it was anything to worry about. Well, I never thought about it either way. When you pointed out that forgetting entire evenings was a bad sign, I realized you might have had a point. But then, like those nights, I forgot about it.

As time in San Francisco wore on, I did take on some of your American habits, like planning for stuff. And the fact that we hadn't truly made any plan when you asked me to come up with you became more and more clear. What were we thinking? Of course, I didn't care at the time. I had already fallen for you and deplored the thought of your leaving alone, and I saw in you a future.

I should have recalled why I had hated Phoenix so much. Maybe I had never put my finger on it. And when those months together turned into a year, I began to feel a dull ache for my family. I didn't say much to you about it because I couldn't imagine a solution to it. I didn't want you to feel bad and I didn't really want to go back, either, so I'd have a few drinks because that's what we did back home, and it let me ignore the ache for a little while.

You never made the connection between that first night when my buddies brought me home and the big date—my visa had expired that day. The vast gate of the two-thousand-mile border had shut then, snuffing out any thought of going home for a visit. Those giant concrete cylinders that comprise the fence along the border became like metal bars in a jail cell. Though nothing had physically changed, the idea of my being with you did—I was no long just with you, but *stuck* with you. Of course, I wanted to be with you. I loved you. I still do. But something that day also sparked a tiny flame of anger in me—not with you—but with the injustice of the world, and the way it forces you to make choices between one thing or the other, never allowing you to have both. Well, you could have both—Americans can do whatever they want and go wherever they please. But for the rest of us, we must choose. I doubted my visa would be renewed. I didn't have the papers to prove my livelihood in Guanajuato. So I stayed with you, happily, and I treated the wounds of longing for home and my family with Corralejo.

We fought sometimes. It was May, nearly five years ago now, and there had been one party after another—May's a patriotic month in Mexico. I'd been working that night shift for well over a year. I had spoken less and less to my family. My sister got married and I couldn't be there for the wedding. And you and I were spending less time together—our schedules of free time never coincided, and then they asked me to work on Sundays, our skating day at Golden Gate Park. By that time, I had become great friends with Chuy and Chepa from the restaurant, and we were regulars at the Esta Noche Bar, especially on Wednesday drag nights. You and I had grown so distant that it seemed at times we hardly knew each other, and I imagined you'd probably gotten tired of me.

I showed up at 4:00 a.m. that Wednesday night, or Thursday morning, I should say. Drunk, drunk, drunk. We had stayed until closing time, when the bartender and the waiter and some drag queen named Valentina suggested we lock the doors and have a private party. The owner had left on some sort of trip and the cops had already been in that week, so we all thought it was a great idea.

I had hardly ever smoked pot, and I'd never tried a stripper pole before, so you can only imagine the two things together after a full night of drinking. I think I sprained a buttock, if that is even possible. I told you later I had fallen down skating. I didn't like to lie, and I had never cheated on you, but even I knew that things between you and me were nearing the brink, and I didn't want to push it any further than I already had.

I had woken you up again, and you couldn't go back to sleep for fretting over me and for being upset. Your face was as red that night as the first day I met you. You'd been angry before, but this time was different. I would never forget it. I was certain that I had finally broken the camel's back, as you sometimes said to me, and I suddenly found myself wondering where I had stored my old duffel bag. It seemed your prediction had come true—the bottle had killed us.

Instead of screaming, you started crying, which suddenly sobered me up, despite my self-destructiveness. You stood up from the bed and started walking toward me, and I opened my arms wide to receive you. I couldn't believe that I had failed you, and I, for once, wanted to take back what I had done, unshoot the Corralejo, and tell you how sorry I was. I didn't do any of those things. Instead we held each other tight and you repeated over and over again, "I love you," while I said, "Te amo, te amo."

You gave me water and led me by the hand to the futon, where we sat as the morning light broke in. You stood by the window and looked out onto treetops and rooftops. "Amor, you have to get ready for work," I said.

You shook your head and started crying again, and then I knew that even though you loved me, you couldn't be with me anymore. I was the problem, I knew, and so I would have to go. You had given me almost two years to make this work, and I couldn't.

"I don't feel like I know you anymore," you told me.

My mouth moved to say something, but even after two glasses of water it still felt too dry to speak.

Then you said, "I'm not going to work."

So you'd spend one last day with me. Maybe you'd see me off to the airport, or make sure I didn't steal any of your things, I figured. You stepped closer. I heard your dreaded words before you said them: *It's best for you to go home.* You put my hands in yours, and my fight left me like my drunkenness. I nodded my head in anticipation. I could no longer look at you. Would I take a bus or a plane, I wondered.

Your speech began with, "I've thought about it… a lot." The pauses between your sentences tortured me. "This isn't working." You were right, I knew you were right. "And I want to start a restaurant with you."

What? Had I been deluded by the liquor?

"Did you hear me?" an angel asked. He was you. You were an angel. And all at once, I believed in you and me again. I felt the pain and anguish dissipate and I knew that we could conquer our demons.

We made love that early morning. We didn't *make* it, actually it was already there between us. We found it, remembered it, and revived it. And in that moment, it seemed ludicrous that we could have ever let it slip away.

IT TURNED out that your 401k only amounted to about a hundred thousand dollars, numbers that even now are hard for me to understand. But you had decided to go all in. The next day, we both quit our jobs, you liquidated assets, and we started hunting for an adequate place for a restaurant. We couldn't have been luckier—"Location, location," you kept saying—and we found a place in the heart of the Mission District, two blocks from the police station, three blocks from Dolores Park, and within walking distance of the Castro for those adventurous queens willing to make the trek for authentic cuisine.

The condition of the place wouldn't qualify as lucky, however, and within a month or two, I learned that Americans are good at spending money. To me, a hundred thousand dollars was a fortune. We could have built a restaurant from the ground up back home, and still had money left over for your precious "cushion of capital." Back home, our construction friends would have put in the tile floor for next to nothing, and mixed the cement and grout with a shovel right outside on the street. In San Francisco, they brought fancy electric equipment, scales for measuring, digital levels, and diamond saws. The guys back home shaped tiles with hand tools and eyeballed the precision of the tile placement, always with a couple of dripping cans of beer nearby.

The guys in San Francisco were all compatriots but they charged like gringos. Before we knew it, almost all of that money was gone. I knew it stressed you out—you would grind your pretty white teeth a lot and rub your forehead. You thought about applying for a loan at the bank. You were all in, almost every penny. And me? I paid for the take-out food and chipped in as much as I could for the household expenses. Pay for undocumented workers falls under the regulations of the employer, not the law. My take-home pay didn't leave me much compared to your former salary.

Poor man, you bore all the pressure, while I was sure we'd make it all back in a few months. That timing turned out to be a bit unrealistic—we did turn a profit after a while, though, and covered the bills. Now your business is worth more than that 401k, although you're still not able to understand that and enjoy what you have. You and I had encountered each other again and the restaurant breathed new life into us—we went from spending no time together to every waking second. We didn't get tired of each other, and we thrived off of one another's excitement. And once we hired Chava, with the troubled life of his and the chance to help him turn things around, we had yet another purpose.

seven

"MOTHAFUCKA left my shit outside on the porch!" Chava said as he walked in the door.

"Good, at least you got your clothes," Joe answered, tired from the day's work. He'd waited up for Chava to show up after dropping by his old place for his things. He'd even halfway crossed himself for Chava as he passed Arturo's crucifix, right before he shook his head at the superstition.

"Put my clothes in a garbage bag! Somebody could have taken it…. I should burn his fuckin' house down."

"No," Joe said as he closed the door tight. "There will be no pyromania tonight. Just get settled in and cleaned up; you smell like garlic. Forget about Dario."

"Sure, whatever. And do you think he's going to forget about me?"

Joe showed him to the guest room. "There's only one bathroom," he said. "It's an old home. We share."

"Better than the park," Chava answered. "I really, you know, like, thank you. You don't have to do this."

"I don't use the space. I'd rather have my head cook close to me, anyhow, and make sure he gets to work on time."

"Don't you be thinkin' I'm yo' bitch, either." His voice rose to a higher pitch and his head jerked from side to side.

"Take it easy. Take it easy." He repeated those three words he'd been using with Chava since the volatile kid was seventeen.

"Take it easy," Chava mocked. "People ought to quit fuckin' with me."

"Here's the bathroom, there's your bedroom. I'm going to bed. Make yourself at home." Joe went across the hall to the bedroom and plopped himself on the bed, leaving the door slightly ajar. His head fell back on the headboard and he started to doze off. He woke up a minute later when Chava opened the medicine cabinet and the toothpaste and razors fell out.

Chava stood across the way, in front of the bathroom sink, in his boxer briefs. After so many years, Joe realized he had never seen the kid naked, or in his underwear, even, not that he should have. Joe was surprised to see that, without his typically baggy clothes and long-sleeved shirts, he had a wiry body, thin but defined. His biceps—"bunnies," as they're called in Mexico—were as big as lemons, and on his chest sprouted a small patch of black hair that ran a thin trail down to his bellybutton. His skin looked smooth and light brown, a perfect, consistent hue except for the distortions of scars on his arms, shoulders, torso, and legs.

His underwear was Calvin Klein, and Joe thought he figured out the reason for Chava not having paid his rent to Dario. What other bills could the kid have? Chava's movements in front of the mirror were girly. As he leaned in close to the mirror, displaying a big green image of the Virgin Mary across his back, Joe assumed he leaned in to inspect the gash on his eyebrow, but then realized he did so to pluck them instead. Chava let out little yelps and crunched up his nose, as he yanked the hairs close to the wound. Joe admired his body, surprised, for some reason, at how good he looked. He peered down at his underwear again, and at the voluptuous package it contained in front. Chava was surely a mix of contradictions, and Joe had never really considered him sexually, seeing him more as a belligerent teen, but seeing the young man nearly naked now aroused him a bit. He hadn't thought about sex for a long while, and hadn't had it since….

Chava caught Joe staring. Joe immediately looked away before he heard, "I ain't yo' bitch, either," followed by the slamming of the bathroom door. Joe felt too tired to be embarrassed. Anyway, sex with Chava, aside from being practically incest, would likely bring nothing but trouble. He reached over to close the bedroom door and fell asleep to the sound of Chava quietly singing Laura León songs in the bathroom: "Yo soy del club de mujeres engañadas"—*I'm from the jilted women's club.*

That night, a *calavera* appeared in Joe's dream. It wasn't a scary or deathly skull, but a cheery, bright one, like the baby blue and white one made of sugar with yellow ribbons on top that Arturo used to put on the *ofrenda*. This one had all the colors of the rainbow, and dangly earrings. Its jaw moved strangely, as if attached by puppet strings, and it spoke to Joe in a muffled, albeit gleeful tone, laughing in between at some things it said, its teeth sort of clattering as it did so. Joe couldn't make much sense of it in the morning, figuring the dream had originated from his thoughts about the upcoming Day of the Dead and the *ofrenda* he would soon design, a shrine to his beloved. He woke up unusually energetic, Chava's being in the other room giving him some motivation for actually making breakfast that day.

The lunch crowd was a bit light for a Thursday. "What do you mean you had breakfast with Chava?" It was Alberto at the other side of the table, the loose roll of skin on his neck shaking incredulously. "He's not even here today."

"I know. We had breakfast at my house."

"At your house?" Alberto leaned in as much as his stomach would allow. "You let him in your house?"

"Yes. He stayed there last night."

"Oh, no. Joe, you're not…."

"No. Nothing like that. He had some problems where he was living, spent a night in the park, and I told him to come over."

"I'm telling you," Alberto said, stuffing a heaping forkful of beans in his mouth, "that kid is problems."

"I'll take my chances."

"It's what I've always told you—you give him too many chances. You shouldn't be mixing personal stuff with business. You're too nice to that kid. He's not learning any discipline by being spoiled all the time. It's codependence, my friend. You've got to learn to draw the line and stick to it."

Joe took a sip of coffee. "I hear you."

"You never know about Chava, and what troubles he might bring. I wouldn't trust him."

"Right. You never know. But we've always thought someone should give him a chance."

"'We'? You're not 'we' anymore. I hate to remind you. And you, both of you, have given Chava years of chances. Learn to draw the line."

Joe nodded with another sip, peering at Alberto, a professional phone counselor, through the steam.

"And what about the other thing, Joe?"

"Which one?"

"You still look weary, maybe today not as much. But you haven't had a break in… how long?"

"I know. Not since… well, it's been a long time. And I don't have anyone to run the restaurant for me, anyway."

"Excuses."

"Maybe. Well, what do you expect, that I'm going to put Chava in charge?"

"Hardly. But one thing is certain—you don't have anyone you can put in charge because you don't want to, not because there's no one out there who could do it. You've been sharing a grave for, what, three years now?"

"Maybe."

"Not maybe. Certainly."

"I'm not ready yet. I still need time. Even you said I've got to do this in my own way and in my own time."

"True. I said that almost three years ago."

"Right."

"Joe." Alberto waited for Joe to look over. "Arturo would have you take care of yourself for a change. Wouldn't he?"

"Yes. Only because he loved me that much. And how am I supposed to let that kind of love go and forget about him?"

"Letting go and forgetting are two different things."

Joe's eyes became teary as he averted Alberto's gaze and stood up. "Yeah," he managed. "Let me get your check."

EIGHT

I HAD waited for Miriam, my little sister, outside the wall of her primary school. At first I stood there, but then got tired and leaned against the wall, and finally sat on the ground, playing with the threads of my light-blue uniform pants at the hem that had been let out a couple of times as I grew. Secondary school had already been excused, and I usually waited the hour for her because Mamá didn't think she was big enough to walk home by herself. Mamá usually came to get us both, so when Miriam came outside we sat there together for a while until I decided no one was coming for us and we'd have to make the walk by ourselves.

The house was a fifteen-minute walk away when we took the back alleys. Mamá didn't like us to go that way because one time some kid slipped on the moss and fell into a dry canal. He broke his leg and the firemen had to come and hoist him out of there, and so Mamá told us to walk on the front roads, the long way by the old temple. Since Mamá wasn't there, I decided we'd go the back way. Anyway, there wasn't any moss, either, and the canal was dry, as always. Miriam got nervous when I started to climb up on the statue of El Pípila, and before I could give the miner's war cry, she started wailing like a baby, so I got down, yanked her hand, and took her home.

Mamá was wailing, too, and that was when we figured out why she had left us at school alone. It hadn't been the first time—once in a while Mamá went to market or lost track of time with her friends over coffee—but this time Grandmother had died. It seemed strange because we were just munching on olives with her the other day, and she walked stiffly, as she had for years, but otherwise seemed to be normal.

Now Mamá cried on the couch and my grandfather sat there blank-faced with a cigarette in his hand. He'd suck on it and then stare straight through the rising smoke, seemingly ignoring all the noise in the rest of the house and that his wife was dead.

The front door was like the opening of an ant nest, with people from all over the town coming in with armloads of food they had made and brought with them. Our house was little, so it got packed really quickly, and the women sort of gathered together in the kitchen while the men huddled around the living room as if they were going to discuss a football play. Nobody said anything to me, but anonymous hands patted my head as I walked by. I went to my bedroom and wondered if I still had to do my homework. Then I realized no one would be giving me big portions of bananas with cream like Grandmother did because my mamá never made them.

I mostly felt alone during the week-long funeral proceedings, except for when I took care of Miriam and tried to answer her questions. All those rituals seemed to be about the adults. Once in a while my mamá told me to go get food from the kitchen—we'd never had so much food—and she'd tell me to serve some for my sister. Even if she'd thought about me, she probably wouldn't have known what to say, or thought to ask how I felt. And I didn't know how I felt.

Months later, something inside me compelled me to get that *calavera* for Grandma. My grandfather had died too, about six weeks after Grandma, and we had a similar string of rituals in the house. I loved him, and I remember the *conchas* he would buy me now and again, but mostly I thought of Grandma. I emptied my piggybank. I didn't want to break it and it didn't have the hole on the bottom to get the money out, so I spent the better part of an evening pulling the coins out one by one with a butter knife. It was more than enough to buy the biggest *calavera* I could find. The yellow ribbons reminded me of an apron she wore most days, and I had associated the light blue of my uniform pants with her death for some reason. More than the colors, the eye sockets in the sugar skull had captured an expression of hers. She would look at me tenderly and quietly with a content grin on her face, and her eyes got big, as if her most desired wish had come true. The big eye sockets were like hers, and the sparkly sugar around them glistened the way her watery eyes did. So I bought it and got a plastic cup of bananas with cream that didn't taste nearly as good as Grandma's had.

As I grew older, I understood the love Grandma and I had for each other. I had always wished I had a way to tell her, or that I had said good-bye to her before her heart attack. I kept the *calavera* safe for some twenty years after that, taking it out only around the second of November, and now I know she felt my love, feels my love, since before her death and ever after.

It's not what I had imagined. Back then, I was so limited by what my mind could comprehend, like a dog listening to the soliloquies of his master. We put so much stake in language and don't even begin to understand its inadequacy. Take "life" or "death." I had never known that a realm spanning the universe exists between those two words. Yet down there on the planet we cling so much to controlling what little is within our grasp. I had made fun of you Americans for micromanagement of detail and fear of letting go, yet, in the larger scheme of things, we were all groveling on the same miniscule grain of sand. We couldn't know.

Even now I use language because I know you need it to understand, but one day you'll interpret the universe without it, like comprehending a book at many levels without reading a single word of it. Different levels of energy and consciousness that you may experience may give you an idea of what is real for me now. It's not an alert level of consciousness, not a wakefulness, either, only an eternal state of being, knowing, and accepting. There is no time or space. But there is feeling, and I feel for you and the pain you make yourself suffer. There is also wisdom which lets me know you are okay and always will be. For your own sake, I hope you'll understand that much. I know you will never get the entirety of my message, mostly because you won't allow yourself.

I am here. Without possessiveness. You are not mine and never were. We actually own nothing, not even our own souls. They are just there. Nobody is separate from anybody else, as here I am with Grandma and my grandfather, your grandparents too, all those mummies, and even the guy from on top of the cliff. You torment yourself, amor, fighting between the love you still have for me and your need to move on. But I am here. You need not move on, you need only move over.

You recall the love we shared and expressed through sex. Even in intimacy we had a shortage of words and an abundance of meaning. The energy we spent, the way we used to sweat, and all the sleep we lost when we felt most in love. Logically, we thought we'd feel tired the next day yet we woke up more energetic than ever. Energy begot energy. Is that why you have brought Chava closer to you?

Here you are, amor, wallowing in a sadness you cannot see beyond. It is a void. One might think you'd be well rested after so much downtime. Instead you've let the emptiness suck away your life force. Yes, learn to rebalance. And learn that I will be here no matter which path you choose. Let the fire consume you again.

NINE

"HOW'D it go?" Alberto asked over his second plate of grilled meat. A paper napkin tucked into his collar reached down to between the first and second buttons. The rest of the shirt would have to fend for itself.

"He's here, isn't he?" With his chin, Joe indicated Chava, who was sweating over the grill.

"Today he is. Tomorrow who knows? I'm telling you... you never know about him. The kid could be trouble." He bit half the meat off a chicken leg.

"You don't mind him today, do you? He's been on the grill all night. He cooked that chicken leg."

Alberto shrugged as Joe stacked dirty plates at his table. "Well, he wouldn't have known that chicken leg was for me. If it wasn't all-you-can-eat *parrilla*, I wouldn't have trusted it."

"I know you don't like him—"

"No. It's not about whether or not *I* like him. It's about what's best for you."

Joe picked up the dirty plates and surveyed the restaurant. Not a table was empty, the floor was filthy, and people stood waiting outside the door. All-you-can-eat night had coincided with the 9th US Circuit Court of Appeals decision a few hours earlier favoring gay marriage, and all the gays and liberals were out to celebrate. "Can't talk now. I gotta get this place clean." He gave the table a quick swirl with a towel which he stuffed back in his apron.

"Mark my words...." Joe heard as he headed to the kitchen.

Señora Darina stood in front of the metal *comal* on which she laid the flattened balls of masa. She concentrated on her work, struggling to keep up with the demand for tortillas. Beside her, Chava worked the barbecue-style grill, the *parrilla*, tongs in one hand and a spatula in the other. To Joe, it sometimes seemed he had a third hand that positioned the plates for the next round of meats. As professional as a grand pianist focusing on his instrument, Chava looked almost butch for a minute, except for the two thin lines he called eyebrows. Chava might have been a mess at times, but he had earned the head cook position on sheer merit. His attendance and disposition were separate issues altogether.

"Dave and Shelley!" Joe yelled out, striking through the names of the next people on the waiting list. A couple appeared from the mob outside, and so did some hipster kid with long straggly hair, who waltzed in and asked how much longer. "If your name's on the list, not more than thirty minutes," Joe answered. "We're working as fast as we can."

The kid turned around to his buddies smoking on the street. "Half a fucking hour, Chainsaw," he said, to the disapproving looks of an older couple and a mother with her children. Joe showed them his agreement with a roll of his eyes as he ushered Dave and Shelley to their table.

It had been months since he'd seen the business thriving like this. Though not exactly clockwork, the waiters and cooks and bartender knew what they were doing. The wait was less than ideal, but the customers consumed their food with delight, and rewarded the hard-working staff with especially generous tips. It reminded Joe of the first couple of years, when Arturo stood in the position that Chava occupied tonight. Arturo had exerted the same concentration, but every now and then would look up to spot his partner, and give him a quick wink or blow him a kiss.

The time Joe had really celebrated was after a meeting with the accountant. "Bravo, José!" she had said to him, "You're all paid off... totally in the black!" He threw the staff an all-night party, handed out bonuses, and got so drunk he had to crawl up the stairs of the flat on hands and knees, Arturo behind him like a dominatrix. He barfed more or less into the toilet before Arturo got him to bed, his head spinning inside like a merry-go-round.

"José," the hostess said, pulling at his sleeve with a distressed look. "We've got a problem," she said to him in Spanish, a sign something was seriously wrong. He glanced over to the door, where the hipsters had entered from the street and now surrounded the podium.

Joe power-walked toward the door. "Yes, sir? Can I help you?"

"We've been waiting for a fucking table forever," the guy said, "and my friend Chainsaw here's getting really pissed off."

"Like I said, we're working as fast as we can. Let me check your name on the list."

"My name's not on the fucking list. We just want a table to get some food. That's all."

"Alright. Try to relax. Maybe we can get you an appetizer and I'll squeeze in your name on the list."

"Why's it taking so long, mister?" He took a step toward Joe as he asked the question, his irritation apparently not diminishing.

"It's all-you-can-eat. We've got a big crowd."

"Look." The guy pointed over to Alberto, whose glance darted away as soon as Joe looked over. "That dude's been here the whole fucking time! He's at a table for four—just enough space for me and my friends. All-you-can-eat? He's had about all anyone should eat! Look at the fat motherfucker!"

"No, sir. He can be at the table as long as he pleases."

But the guy ignored Joe and stepped over to the table as his three friends clad in torn black surrounded the table. Alberto looked up at them with his mouth open, grease on his lips, and a piece of flank steak on his fork.

"Time to go, fat ass!" the first one said.

"Yeah, porky, your time's up. It's all-you-can-eat, not all-everyone-can-eat," said the one called Chainsaw.

Joe tried to squeeze in between two of them, but they were like immobile pillars. He figured it was time to call the police. He headed for the podium, and then stared blankly at the base of the wireless phone. Where was it?

He turned around to see the four guys closer yet to Alberto, who had slid back a foot or so in the chair. Their fingers jabbed at him as he uselessly attempted to bat them away. He tried to sit forward in the chair, but the guys pushed him back, until finally his foot slipped and he fell faceup on the floor.

"Get out!" they yelled at him.

Then one landed a heavy black boot on the big man's ribcage. Alberto let out a cry.

"Call the cops!" someone shouted. Joe knew they'd never get here in time. They were probably up on Castro Street dealing with the citywide celebration, or down at City Hall.

Two of the hipsters bent down to grab Alberto by the arms. "Let's haul his ass out of here!"

"Get off of him, you mothafuckas!" came a high-pitched voice. The quartet froze for a second and their gazes veered over to Chava, whose pin-striped eyebrows slanted in a protective pose. He held up a bloody knife the size of a machete and waved it with determination in his eyes. "Come on, boys, give me one reason to cut you, or else get the fuck out!"

Chainsaw let go of Alberto and lifted his hands in surrender as the other three made a beeline for the door. When the door closed behind the last hipster, applause erupted around Chava, who lowered the long knife to his hip. A huge smile came across Joe's face, and the memory of the crowd at the Alley of the Kiss came instantly to his mind. He knelt down to Alberto as the hostess rushed to give Chava a hug. "Are you okay?" Joe asked, grabbing Alberto's hand.

From where he lay on the floor, Alberto looked around at the many staring eyes. He only nodded. Then Chava and Joe and the hostess hoisted Alberto back up into the chair. Alberto looked at Chava, apparently unsure what to say, so summing it up with a jovial smile.

"Ain't nobody gonna be nobody's bitch around here," Chava said to Alberto. "We stick together.... We is who we is... and we family."

And then he turned around and walked back to the kitchen as if nothing had happened.

Joe leaned in to Alberto. "Now, what was it you were saying about Chava?" Alberto remained speechless. "You never know about him, right?"

Joe wiped his hands on his apron and then raised them up to try to calm the clientele. *Another day in the Mission,* he thought.

Before he got back to work, the hostess approached him. "Here's the phone you were looking for, Joe. It was ringing off the hook—not for reservations, just some jerk who kept crank-calling. He said, 'You're gonna pay' in a creepy voice and then he'd hang up."

TEN

A PAINTING in our living room that had been there as long as I could remember depicted a young man wrapped in the Mexican flag plunging to his death from the rooftop of a castle. His face had the stoic expression of a true patriot, a defiant martyr, and the peach fuzz of an adolescent boy. As was the norm in my town, framed pictures were always hung much closer to the ceiling than the floor—I hadn't taken much notice of the painting until I was ten or eleven. Once I had, I found it rather eerie, this kid not much older than me falling to his certain death.

"Who threw the boy off the roof of that castle?" I asked Mamá.

"What?" she asked, confused, until she saw me standing on a dining room chair, analyzing the picture. "Oh, him. Nobody threw him off. He jumped."

"Why, Mamá? Why would he jump?"

"For the Americans."

Accustomed to short answers to my questions—all adults were alike in that—I tried to figure it out from the image. The boy wore a soiled military uniform, his dark-blue jersey and white pants showing from beneath the folds of the flag. Smoke and cannon fire were behind him. Troops in olive drab stormed in, crashing through the castle portal. I imagined myself atop the castle, hurling myself over the wall. I needed to know.

"Are these the Americans?" I pointed to the ones in green.

"Yes."

"And why were they after these children?"

Mamá chuckled. "They weren't children, 'Turo, they were cadets in the military school."

"And?"

"Didn't they teach you about those cadets in school?"

I shrugged. Mamá stopped her sweeping to give me the long answer for once and for all. She put her hand on the top of the broom handle like a soldier grabbing his rifle by the muzzle. "I think it was 1850 or so, and the Americans were mad about the Alamo. They wanted our land, just like the Spaniards and French. They might have thought to earn a day's living instead of stealing it. That gold in California was ours!

"Anyway, their troops made it down to Mexico City, and they headed for the Chapultepec Castle. Maybe they thought the president was there or something. Instead, it was a bunch of kids—young men who had signed on to the army since... about your age.

"But those kids, six of them, had the courage of grown men. They fought off hundreds of gringos for hours. They refused to surrender or retreat. Finally, the gringos got the upper hand. As they battered their way into the castle, that one"—she pointed at the boy in the picture—"Juan Escutia (*I* paid attention in history class), did not want the flag to fall into enemy hands. He wrapped himself in it and escaped them, along with the symbol of our country, and leapt to his death."

I stood on the chair, enthralled with her story.

"They are called the Niños Héroes, the Boy Heroes. And I respected them ever since I learned about them in school. Even young people like you can sacrifice everything for what they believe in and for what they love. Sometimes I've seen the way you take care of your sister. You watch out for her. That's heroic."

"Oh, Mamá, that's not the same as fighting off Americans or jumping off a building."

"I don't care. You are a good kid. You try hard, except maybe in history class. You are my boy hero."

I had never thought of gringos as the enemy. I could hardly imagine battalions of Americans tramping all the way down to Mexico City to attack a military school. Indeed, the United States had always seemed like a sort of Promised Land, a land of fortune, and a prohibited one too. Most everyone respected the gringos who visited Guanajuato, or at least the dollars they would bring, though most Americans who would make it down our way seemed different from the gabachos I'd see shouting and dancing embarrassingly on the beach with noses painted white and hair dyed blond. None of them behaved like enemies. Imbeciles, maybe.

I had known a lot of people who had gone to the United States in search of work. Some of them made it and would deposit generous sums in family accounts or send telegrams and money through Western Union. Others came back sooner than expected, detailing the trials they had suffered, and the bursting of the great American illusion. Yet I could never put a face on that despot or ruler who wanted so desperately to keep us out. Was it that guy Uncle Sam? Because his girlfriend, the Statue of Liberty, had a different opinion, didn't she?

As a boy, my image of the US was of big houses and broad highways with bridges all over the place. Everything was clean, all the people were smart and white, and they all drove nice cars. In their wallets they had loads of cash and credit cards and could buy whatever they wanted. Every street had a huge mall with glass ceilings and indoor fountains. And every city had an amusement park with gigantic roller coasters and dizzying teacups and wild animals that would jump on your fancy car. Everything in the United States was great in my mind, but it was all separated from us by this big thing they called La Línea—The Line. Strange a line could make such a difference... kind of like when people would draw a line in the sand or Mamá, in order to resolve a territory conflict between my sister and me, would say, "Don't cross this line—this is her side, that is your side."

After Mamá's explanation of that picture, I could imagine all those guys in green standing on the other side of the line, ready to shoot any boy wrapped in a flag who might jumping over it. The people back home called them "La Migra." Some of those friends who left for the US got caught by La Migra and thrown back into Mexico like garbage bags on Tuesday mornings. Other people left and nobody ever heard from them again, as if they were swallowed up by The Line or La Migra, and never spit out. I guess I'd rather be the garbage. And a few people who left ended up living up there. They became Americans and forgot they were ever Mexicans. Their families would hear from them less and less and those generous bank deposits would taper off too. Maybe they were too busy getting their cars and houses and stuff.

I had never planned to go to the United States, not to live and work, anyway. I was intimidated by The Line and La Migra with their green uniforms and helicopters and guns. After I graduated from preparatory school, I applied for my tourist visa because everyone else did. They said we'd all go to Magic Mountain or Epcot. Nobody got a visa except for me. I guess it was my lucky day because we all compared our paperwork—bank statements, report cards, blank records of criminal histories, and the like. None of us was particularly rich, had special connections, or negative histories. I got mine, theirs got denied, all ten or twelve of my friends' applications. I guess the girl at the consulate had met her quota of approvals for the day—one—so she rubberstamped the rest "denied." They were mad at me. Once I got the actual visa card, I stuck it in a secret place in my room, mentally scratched off any plans for a trip to the US, and went on to the university. I'd have gone to the US on borrowed money anyway. As far as I could see, that visa would sit there for its span of ten years, and then I'd take my chances at renewing it.

A lot can change in ten years. Architecture, tourism, pedagogy, and computers—my four choices at the university. No, no, no, and no. I took architecture because it was the only one I had any interest in—at least I could appreciate the art and history of it that was all around me in Guanajuato. But concrete mixtures, technical drawings, and weight-bearing points? Ugh. I hated it. Perhaps if the instructors had cared much about teaching, I might have been more motivated. When the tests came up, it seemed like the theory instructor was out to get us for not having "applied" ourselves or shown "respect." I think he should have arrived on time like he expected us to, but he had the authority. The copies of the handwritten exam were practically illegible, and two people got thrown out for asking each other what the questions said. That didn't matter much—only three people in our whole group passed the exam. We'd have to repeat the course with same instructor. Another guy in the group suggested we go up to Phoenix. We'd learn English and would come back with tons of dollars, and he already had a job lined up. I dropped out of the university, went to Phoenix for almost a year, and I came back after hating it, with a serious tan and a few dollars, not tons, to figure out what I'd do for the rest of my life.

In Guanajuato, I worked at whatever I could find besides manual labor—I hated the hard work in Phoenix—and I helped out at home between jobs. I hoped to land a government job but they officially required a bachelor's degree and, unofficially, either a higher-up who was a blood relative or a sufficient bribe. I had none of those. My family had lived in Guanajuato forever, but we were humble folks, unconnected to politics or big business. We were always content with our families and friends who would get together practically every weekend for birthdays and anniversaries and Cervantino preparations.

I hadn't fallen in love, either. It was a small, traditional town. People would talk. Though I didn't really think my parents would mind, I didn't want to come out of the closet and embarrass them. My sexuality was like a disregarded shirt tucked back in a drawer, not necessarily because it was despised or anything, but because it didn't seem to fit right. It clashed. So it stayed in the back of the drawer, relatively forgotten.

I did have a couple flings in the hills and in the hushed darkness of someone's bedroom, nothing more than sexual exploration. I had no interest in the opposite sex. And then you came along and changed everything, and I wondered how I could be with you and still be Mamá's boy hero.

ELEVEN

JOE stayed in the restaurant past midnight with a bunch of celebrators. It occurred to him that the same ruling might have made a world of difference to him way back when, but meant little to him now. But he didn't want to spoil anyone's fun, or be considered a grouchy war victim complaining about people's basking in the glory of gay matrimony for which he had suffered. Instead, he gave out free shots of house tequila to all those happy gay and lesbian couples who sported matching wedding rings—those who married in what turned out to be the eight-month window of gay liberation between Marriage Equality Laws, Proposition 8, and the ensuing ping-pong game of appeals.

One of those couples had sent the "gorgeous" cook a twenty-dollar tip with strict directions that it not be inserted in any sort of communal tip jar, but be given to the young man personally. Chava left with them after his shift, promising to be home before morning. Joe reserved any opinion about it. Indeed, Chava had turned the ugly situation with Alberto into a triumphant one. What might have scared away customers ended up solidifying their loyalty. Joe realized he could have taken preventive action before it ever got that far, but he didn't want to be accused of stereotyping. No matter how you sliced it, unpleasant customers were a staple of all restaurants. Joe felt grateful to Chava. He gave him a key to the house and, tonight at least, would let him do whatever he wanted.

Shortly after the incident with the hipsters, Alberto had slipped out quietly, not an easy feat for a man of his size. He left two twenties on the table under a plate of food he had left there, having not touched another bite after regaining his composure. Sad, Joe thought, the man going home by himself after such a humiliation. He doubted anyone could look at him and refrain from judgment. True, the man was skilled at listening and giving out advice—he was a phone counselor, after all—but he didn't seem to have much ability to take any.

At the start of their friendship, Joe had suggested he get out a bit, tame the consumption, and take care of himself. Alberto responded with a curt, "Mind your own business," and so that's what Joe tried to do. After Chava's "Al Puerco" insult, Joe noticed how quickly the man could turn on someone—perhaps his method of drawing boundaries—and nobody liked to be called a pig. Joe couldn't really attest to the strength of their friendship, if that's what they had. The extent of their knowing each other was nothing more than conversations, hundreds of them, over many plates of food and cups of coffee. Joe didn't even have his phone number. What kind of friend was that? In reality, neither he nor Joe were about to play a match of tennis or even take walks in the park together—Joe because of the restaurant and Alberto due to his weight. Yet now that he pondered it, he concluded Alberto was a friend after all, because friends knew each other and accepted each other. And he wished he had been a better friend, because he wondered now if Alberto would ever come back.

In the dark night, Joe walked over to Noe Valley all alone. Arturo had pointed out that "Noe" was Spanish for Noah, which made Joe envision all the pairs of homosexuals who, walking hand in hand, might just reach an ark and be saved from forty days, or forty years, of conservative flooding. "Noe's Ark"—the perfect name for a gay bar in the neighborhood.

The night seemed peaceful for a Friday, and the October air felt fresh and hospitable. It had been a while since he'd felt the satisfaction of a good day's work. He crossed the street, stepping into a pothole in the asphalt. Arturo used to complain about the potholes and power outages, graffiti on walls and drunks in the street. Arturo had come with some notion that everything was perfect in the United States—every crack repaired and every manhole covered. Surely Phoenix hadn't been much better, but Arturo's bias had persisted.

On the other side of the street a street lamp was out, and the darkness was almost black beneath the added shade of a tree. He heard a scuff behind him, somebody's footstep, but he was too tired to care. There was nothing unusual about people walking around late, especially on a Friday night. He heard a footstep again, this time closer, and he turned to look. People do get mugged in San Francisco, and fag-bashed once in a while too. Nobody was visible. He stopped walking and stood on the sidewalk in the blackness under the tree. "Hello?"

No one answered. Nothing unusual about hearing footsteps, but certainly something unusual about not seeing from whom they came. He shook it off and hurried home, working the key in the doorknob quickly. He closed the door behind him and pulled the shade back to peer outside. Was he seeing ghosts? Arturo? Well, here at home he knew just where the phone would be sitting and would be able to call 911 instantly. He went upstairs, shucked off his clothes and the bout of paranoia, and hopped into bed in anticipation of another busy workday tomorrow.

The phone startled Joe awake. He lifted his head from his pillow and saw through squinting eyes the morning light piercing through the window. It had to be at least six or seven. Chava would either be home by now, though Joe had not heard him come in, or asleep some place. He found the phone by the fifth or sixth ring and answered with a groggy hello.

"Joe?" He didn't recognize the voice.

"Yes?"

"Why'd you take him?"

Joe sat up. "Excuse me? Take whom?"

"You can't have him. He's mine," the angry voice continued.

"What are you talking about?"

"Fucking faggot! Rich restaurant owner! He's half your age, pervert. You'll pay for this, alright!"

Joe nearly slammed the phone down until he realized the person on the other end had already hung up. "Unlisted number," the screen read. What the hell? Was this about Chava?

He got out of bed and stormed down the hall. He knocked on the guestroom door and opened it at the same time. "Chava!" he said to an empty, unmade bed. And then, "Damn you."

At ten thirty, the restaurant relatively quiet for a Saturday morning, Chava strolled in. A burgundy hickey accented his neck and another peeped from his chest under the collar of his A-shirt. He smiled on his way in, still glowing, perhaps from yesterday's triumph or else whatever his nocturnal activities might have been.

"You're late again, Chava," Joe said, taking in the face of the wall clock and then Chava's.

"Sorry, boss. Meant to be back home. Meant to be on time." He walked around the kitchen counter, pulling an apron from a hook.

"Sorry?" Joe repeated, exasperated.

"Yeah. I'm sorry. I'm here now, right? Big night yesterday. Stayed up late, alright?"

"This is going too far, Chava."

"Look, Joe, it's still quiet. Me and everybody else in the city stayed out late. Mad 'cause you weren't invited, or what? A girl's got to live a little... and no one's keeping you from havin' some fun yourself."

"You said you'd be back before morning."

"Things changed. I stayed with them. Problem? Just because you let me stay in your house, don't make you my amá."

"True," Joe said, "but I am your boss and I need to talk to you right now."

"José, I got work to do. Take it easy. Let me do my shit."

"Now, I said." He pointed to the corner booth.

Chava dropped his shoulders and his head drooped. "Serious?"

"Now."

Chava came out from the kitchen like the defiant teenager. He crossed his arms as he sat in the booth. "What?"

"If I've told you once I've told you a thousand times—you've got to get here on time. It's a bad example for the other employees."

"Well, it's not like anyone follows my example," he retorted.

"And another thing—you said you'd be back by morning. You had me worried," Joe lied.

"No one asked you to stay up waiting, did they? Besides, that's home, this is work."

"Of course we shouldn't mix the two."

"No, we shouldn't. Home is home, work is work."

"Then who keeps crank-calling both work and home? Is it that Dario? And what's up with that? I thought he asked you to leave for not paying the rent. Sounds like there's more to it than that. Something's got him angry."

Chava's mouth opened in shock. He closed it tight, and his tiger fangs came out again. "None of your business," he spit.

Joe clenched his teeth. "Chava. Now, you better be on the level with me or...."

"Or what? Yo' gonna kick me out? Fire me?"

"Yeah... I'm gonna fire you. I should have long ago."

Chava stood up from the table, his fists clenched. He dug a hand into his front pocket and presented a key, the same bronze key Joe had given him the day before. He smacked it down on the table. "I knew you didn't mean it when you opened your door." Then he untied the apron behind his back and plopped it in a lump beside the key. With his head at full sway, he said, "Arturo was the one who really cared. And I don't need yo' bullshit charity no mo' or yo' sorry-ass fathering. Fuck you." He gave a left-face and marched out the door.

Joe took a deep breath and looked around, suddenly feeling self-conscious in front of the people around him. The workers carried on nonchalantly, perhaps hoping not to be the next called over to the corner booth. Were those the limits Alberto had been talking about? Oh sure, they worked like a charm—put Chava right back in his place. If only Alberto had been here to see how well his free therapy had functioned. Now Joe needed to call in a replacement for Chava. Pangs of guilt surged inside him as he doubted his manner of handling the situation. Had he done the right thing? Sooner or later, he'd known he'd have to put his foot down, and he also knew Chava was never going to make it easy. Joe was more curious than ever what Alberto would have to say this time.

By early evening, Alberto hadn't shown. Joe couldn't remember the last time that he had missed lunch at José Arturo Amor. Joe had hoped the incident with Alberto might blow over without needing another word. And now he felt empty somehow, lonely, realizing how much these two people he'd seen most every day, and whom he'd taken for granted, were now missed. He thought he'd learned a lesson about cherishing loved ones after Arturo disappeared. *People seem to be quite pathetic*, he thought, *when it comes to remembering the most basic rules of life.*

TWELVE

A FEW months after Grandma and my grandfather died, my mother began to ruminate about my first confession. "I think it's time, Papá. No?" she'd say at dinner, only responded to with one of his grunts. Some of my friends had been confessing for years—a few of them really needed to—and others still hadn't. No predetermined date marked the official time for this rite of passage, unlike a baptism on baby's first birthday, First Communion when you're eight, a *quinceañera* on a girl's fifteenth birthday, or a wake once you're dead. "Yes. You must heal your soul," Mamá concluded. I wondered if I had done something wrong.

For the next week or two, I tried to make a mental inventory of bad deeds I had committed—my sins. I almost thought it would be easier to go and purposely break someone's window or kick a cat to relieve myself of any doubt. I thought of the wooden box in the church. I had seen it so many times during Mass and other times we went to the basilica. The box was only open for confession on certain days, so you didn't have to feel bad about your sins until then. Would I reach high enough when I knelt, I wondered, for the padre to see me?

Mamá explained the whole process to me, as did Isaac, a friend at school. I heeded Isaac's words more than Mamá's. "Just tell him you disobeyed the teacher or didn't do your chores," he said. "He'll tell you to say Hail Mary's, to apologize to the teacher, and to clean your room."

I had a nasty thought about Isaac then, and wondered if I should confess it. That kind of reprehensible sin was not confessable, of course. What would the padre think? He'd surely tell Mamá, despite her having said, "Whatever you say is between the padre and yourself. No one will know." I never believed that, so I decided I'd stick to the basic kind of sin.

"Should I tell him I spent my lunch money on Choco Roles after school?" I asked her, to help narrow it down.

"Weren't you hungry at lunch time?"

"Not really. And the boys asked me to play soccer to even out the teams."

"Do you feel bad about it?" she asked.

"No. I feel good about it. I like Choco Roles. And I brushed my teeth later."

"You're supposed to buy a tostada or a torta."

"I know."

"No, don't tell him that. Tell him what you feel bad about."

"And then what?"

"Then he'll give you penance, you'll do it, and you'll be reconciled."

"What's 'reconciled'?"

"You'll be washed clean."

I didn't quite understand where the cleanliness came in, though I always knew it couldn't be from the holy water everyone stuck their hands into. I imagined a soapy scouring pad taken to my insides.

"Just like that? It all turns from bad to good?" It seemed a tad magical.

"Yes. God forgives the penitent."

"What's that?"

"People who are sorry for what they did."

"Okay… I'm sorry." I still wasn't sure exactly for what, or why I had to tell a man. "Could I tell him I got a drink of water from the water jug after Señora Gómez told me to drink from the hose?"

Mamá's face always grimaced when I mentioned the school dean, with whom Mamá had argued a few times over the reasonableness of certain school rules, like drinking from unfiltered water hoses or demanding pricy new uniforms from poor folks. "Tell the padre what you think is right."

Confused again. I'd been looking for things that were wrong.

When the day finally came, Mamá had ironed my best pants and promised to make spicy *birria* of mutton for the whole family with fresh tortillas, lemon wedges, and diced cilantro and onions. Of course, before we ate, I'd have to confess, and change my pants—the burgundy-colored *birria* salsa stained worse than pomegranate.

"Forgive me, padre, for I have sinned. This is my first confession." I had rehearsed it a hundred times, and prepared a mental list of sins. I figured ten would be good enough. For a minute, as I sat in the box, I thought the padre had fallen asleep. I wondered if my sins had bored him. For a second I thought he had died because, even though I couldn't see him in the wooden box, everyone knew he was a really old man. When I heard his wheezing, I continued.

The first nine sins were mundane. The last was my grand finale. "And I pushed Isaac's sister over and called her a butt face for making my little sister cry." That fat girl had it coming for picking on a girl two grades younger than she and half her size. I didn't actually think or feel it was wrong, but I knew I wasn't supposed to push people or call them bad names. Even in my childhood I realized distinguishing right from wrong wasn't as simple as grownups made it seem. In reality, I had embellished my list, because I didn't think I had committed many real sins, those things that truly bad people do because they're evil.

I waited for some recrimination or scolding from the padre. There was a short pause when I had finished. I think he leaned forward a little because I could hear him more clearly. He cleared his throat. "Four Hail Marys, study for your test on your own, and apologize to the girl you pushed." He slid the little door closed so I would know my turn was over. Fifteen minutes later, after my knees had stiffened a bit on the pew, I had finished my penance. My soul was cleansed from its filthy state. I would go to heaven instead of hell. I wasn't about to apologize to the fat girl, and that way I'd get a head start on things I could confess for the next time.

People do love their neat dichotomies: good and bad; black and white; hero and villain. It makes life more manageable. You will either go to heaven or hell. The obvious trouble is that every good guy has a bad side and every bad guy has a good side. What does that leave us? A bunch of guys.

Ay, amor, you torment yourself with right and wrong, judging yourself more harshly than anyone else would if they could read your thoughts or know your feelings. I wasn't much different, though even at that first confession I picked up on the flaws of it all.

Now I realize there aren't two sides—no good and bad, no heaven and hell. I now can see far more than two dimensions. Indeed, there are no sides at all. It's like a never-ending sphere, an infinite mass of ethereal energy, both encompassing you, and everything, and penetrating you as well. If you could know it and meet me here, or let the spark of awareness jump the gap, you'd instantaneously understand. You cannot comprehend it now. There are only a few—mostly monks or psychics out there—who can both collect their energy in a saturated singularity and then open the walls of their souls, as with osmosis, to transfer, receive, and exchange that energy with the universe around them. Your time will come when you are ready. Your energy is becoming more concentrated, amor, but not yet focused.

The energy festers inside crudely—a concentrated blob. Prayer is a way of siphoning it, letting the pressure seep out like a carefully placed pinhole in a balloon. The energy, pushed and pulled as with magnets, or bent as with light and gravity, gets released out there and becomes part of here. You tolerated my insistence on prayer and Mass all those years. I was no fanatic, but I did feel a certain calling, perhaps nothing more than custom, particularly on "sacred" days—Christmas, Good Friday, the anniversary of Grandma's death. You pray more than you think. I don't mean the rote prayers like those that used to give me aches in my knees. For aches in my knees, I would have preferred Isaac. You might not kneel and recite a catechism lesson, but in your own way you interact with something at a different level than your own, one you're finding more and more spiritual. You're starting to relieve the concentration, amor, and share it.

THIRTEEN

JOE wiped a putty spatula on a towel before he folded the cloth to use it as a pad beneath his knees. He believed in hands-on management—he didn't expect his employees to do anything he wasn't willing to do. Hence, he cooked, cleaned, bussed, and waited tables like the rest of them. Now he found himself scraping gum from the bottom of the tables. Perhaps a new city ordinance should replace the old ashtrays with new gumtrays, since smoking was no longer permitted. The gum came in every color of the rainbow, like those on Arturo's serape—mostly peppermint white and turquoise wintergreen, but there was a blue berry, a red cinnamon, and a new one, radiant orange.

He scraped it off, trying to disassociate his disgust from his motions. The color was similar to that of his favorite royal creatures. He sat straight up, took in the fading mural on the far wall, and recalled the day he proclaimed, "Monarch butterflies!"

When they had been brainstorming decorating ideas for the restaurant, most of Joe's ideas had been nixed for one reason or another. But he made his proclamation with such enthusiasm that either everyone on the crew loved the idea or they would have felt too guilty not to act as if they did. Guanajuato hadn't been Joe's first trip to Mexico. He'd also had the chance to go to Michoacán and see the butterflies once they made it home to their mountainous breeding grounds.

Beautiful creatures—no wonder King William III had loved them so much. Each one was a flying Tiffany with black lines and orange panes adorned by unique white specks along its trim. High up in the Sierra Madre near Angangueo, Michoacán, they gathered in such multitudes that they pulled down the mighty limbs of the full-grown pine trees so that the pine needles swept the ground like the bristles of brooms. Hundreds of thousands of people went to see their magnificence every year.

Their beauty was unparalleled, yet the awe that Joe felt was not for their physical appearance but their mystery. Like geese and whales, the butterflies migrated south from as far north as Canada. Unlike the birds and waterborne mammals, none of the butterflies lived long enough to make the entire trip. Somehow, the succeeding generation, born somewhere along the route, knew where to go. How?

Scientists explained the phenomenon as instinct. The butterflies were born with the geographical knowledge. Joe had long respected the ability of science to answer the great questions of the universe and explain how things happen or work, as with dark matter, conception, and Velcro. But after thinking and thinking about it, he couldn't simply swallow "instinct." *It's like the way a baby knows how to suckle*, someone had said once. *Sure*, he thought, *but you can't set a baby down in Canada and tell it you'll meet it in Angangueo, Michoacán, at the fourth tree from the summit.* So they said "trace intelligence," like morsels of information passed on through DNA. It still didn't seem right—science had already explained inception as starting from a single cell. Where was the gray matter, then, in that single cell? Where did the trace intelligence fit? A mystery. To Joe, there was something cool about it, partly because nobody could explain it.

Perhaps religious folks were onto something, he thought. Scientists were smart and all, but they always hoped for answers by looking ever closer. They utilized more powerful lenses, electron microscopes, and particle smashers. Maybe the answers weren't to be found in the microscopic, but in the macro. Perhaps instead of looking inside, one should focus outside. Instead of minute detail, the big picture. Those religious folks peered up and called it God, and then they used religion for all sorts of other distasteful purposes. Still, some answers were better explained from a different, broader perspective. The monarch butterflies knew where to go because of a guiding system greater than what could be seen.

More gum on the tables. Couldn't anyone ask for a tissue? Joe sighed, the excitement of the past few days winding down, and the old feelings coming up again. Maybe those monarch butterflies could lead him to a place where somebody could aptly respond to his lingering doubt: maybe he should have never let Arturo go. He could have prevented all of this. It was his fault.

"Do you want some help?"

Joe lifted his head to see Chava's crotch beside him, his scabby arm dangling at one side, his fingernails freshly polished. "Not with those nails, honey. You're going to chip your press-ons." A genuine, involuntary smile came across Joe's face.

"These ain't no press-ons, baby," answered Chava, swinging his head, his face reflecting Joe's smile. "This is the real shit. What you see is what you get. Okay?"

"You came back." Joe's expression became serious.

"What's that saying about dogs eating the hand that bites them?"

"'Don't bite the hand that feeds you,' I think you mean."

"Yeah, that one."

"But you ain't no one's bitch, right?"

"No, not no bitch. But maybe a dog at times."

Joe stood up and showed off his cup of discarded gems. He towered over Chava.

"I... I didn't mean it. You know? Got mad...."

Joe could see how awkward the moment was for Chava. "Why don't we take it to the booth again?" he said gently.

"Alright."

"I'm glad you're back."

They slid into the booth. Joe surveyed the rest of the staff, nonchalantly working again, but with nearly imperceptible grins on their faces.

"I need to know what's going on... and why that guy keeps calling."

"It's nothing I can't handle."

"I don't care... I need to know—"

"I'm trying to tell you." Chava paused a moment, clearly trying to keep himself calm. "I met Dario a few years ago, when things were going bad with my ex-ex, remember?"

"There have been a lot of them," Joe said matter-of-factly.

"Um... Gene, the upholstery guy."

"Okay."

"Well, in a way, I only needed a place to stay. And I had already met Seth, my ex. You met him, the bear."

"Shaved-head Seth? Tight jeans?"

"Yeah. So Seth was cool, but he kept saying he was tired of San Francisco and wouldn't I leave with him to Seattle or Sydney or someplace. And I said, 'Fuck that, I ain't leaving from my homies,' you know, you and Arturo?"

"Oh. Okay." Goosebumps formed on Joe's arms for a moment, making his arm hair stand up straight.

"So Seth did. He took off. Anyway, I was getting tired of him 'cause he didn't like when I'd go hang out with Dario. We'd get high and shit, or drink a little, and Seth was more like orgasmic."

"Orgasmic?"

"Yeah... like he wanted to eat all healthy food and vegetables."

"Organic."

"Yeah. So Seth had asked me if I wanted his apartment 'cause he could sign it over to me. And I said hell no, 'cause there was no way I could pay sixteen hundred dollars for a stupid little apartment. I don't care if it had a chimney. But then I was like, where am I gonna stay? And Dario said with him."

"You hadn't said anything about Seth leaving you alone like that. I thought you had decided to move."

"I know. It's 'cause that was around the time Arturo had left and hadn't come back. And you were like starting to freak out."

"Uh-huh," Joe said, not having considered this point. Once Arturo had gone, Joe knew his focus had shifted, become lost.

"So Dario said I could stay with him in his apartment down by Market Street."

Joe curled his lip, thinking about the Tenderloin, not his favorite part of the city.

"I know," Chava responded, "but I'm a ghetto girl, okay? I've seen worse. Anyhow, so everything was cool and shit, and I had told him okay, and thanks, but only like friends. And he said that was cool."

"Listen," Joe interrupted, "you don't have to tell me everything. I just need to know how much of a threat he is to you or me, or the house."

"Oh." Chava sat back in the bench, thinking. "Threat? Are you kidding. He's a total pussy. There was this one time we were kissing out in the street by his apartment, and these two lanky-ass black dudes came and started saying shit, right?

"So I put my hat sideways and asked them like what the fuck, you know, did they want to start something. And Dario kind of pulled back on my jacket and said let's go.

"I don't back down. So I come up to them, and before you know it, someone throws a blow, and pulls Dario into it. I mean, he got hit one time and he was down. I'm telling you—he's a total pussy. Then one of those dudes, dark mothafucka, pulls a knife. I look back—Dario splits. The black dude says, 'Faggot, ain't yo' gonna run after yo' boyfriend?' I wasn't gonna be chased off by those dudes in the hood and then be afraid to walk outside every day after that. You got to earn respect, you know? I did what anyone would do—I pulled my knife. I started showing off a little, like in the movies, kind of like Bruce Lee with his nunchucks. They watched me and didn't say nothin'. So I freeze, got the knife out, ready, and I says, 'Bring it on.'

"That dark one looks at his knife—fuckin' steak knife, dude, he probably stole from his mama's kitchen. And he turns to the other one and looks back at me and says it's cool. And they walk off.

"I was all pumped and ready for them. So I yell, 'Go fuck each other, then!' You know they prob'ly did. And I didn't see them around there no more."

Chava stopped and put his hands on the table, indicating the end of the story. Joe sat there in silence, trying to absorb it all.

"Aren't you scared to die like that one night out in the street?" Joe asked. "People get killed over stupid comments."

"It's called pride."

"Is that what your life's about? Is it worth it?"

"I don't know what my life's about, but it ain't worth much."

Ouch. Joe felt sudden pity for Chava, or perhaps empathy—it didn't seem very long ago he might have said the same phrase about his own life. He tried to shake it off and change the subject. "Go back a second. Kissing in the street? I thought you said you were just friends."

Chava shrugged. "Man, you know how it is. Friends, sleeping in the same bed, you get high, he gets horny. He wanted it one time, took it. I couldn't say no—it was his house and I was like drunk. I didn't care. I was kinda horny too. So whatever."

"Whatever? Now he seems to be after you… or us."

"He's a coward, I said. He won't do nothin'."

"Obviously, he's mad, or jealous. He's making phone calls."

"He gonna stab you over the phone?"

"I take it you owe him money?"

"He never told me to pay no rent, until one time I told him again we were only friends, and I went and slept on the floor by his dirty clothes. And he says I better start paying my share."

"And did you?"

"Man, I gave him a little, but I didn't have much to give him."

"Chava, I know you make money. I pay you every two weeks."

Chava lifted his hand off the table and crossed at his chest. "None of yo' business, alright. I got things I got to pay."

Joe considered the stern look on Chava's face. He recalled Chava's CK underwear, and wondered who had paid for all the liquor and drugs. He didn't want to make anything worse, not after this open conversation. "Fine. Let's just make sure we don't have any more trouble from Dario."

"Okay. Are we cool, then? I mean, I swear, I'll try to be on time. I swear."

"Alright. I'm glad you came back."

"Can I go to work, then?"

"Sure."

"By the way, what happened to *Al Puerco*?"

"You mean Alberto?"

"Yeah… is he okay?"

"Not sure. He hasn't come back yet. Now, get to work!"

Chava got up and headed toward the kitchen.

"One more thing," Joe added.

"Yeah?"

"I need you to make the crepe paper cutouts you always make."

"Of butterflies? For Arturo's *ofrenda*?"

"Right."

"No problem."

FOURTEEN

CREPE paper banners had been strung across streets, wooden matracas spun over people's heads like noisy helicopters, meter-long sparklers waved and tossed, mariachi horns and tubas and accordions played in the town center, happy people were everywhere with children on shoulders and older folks beside them with canes and walkers. Not the Cervantino Festival, but New Year's. The streets of Guanajuato weren't as packed, and tourists didn't come from all over the nation or all over the globe—every place would have their own celebration. So the glee this time had a local flavor, townspeople who passed good and bad times together, families who welcomed visiting members returning home for the holidays, and longtime friends and neighbors sharing the union of one year ending and another beginning. The joy and camaraderie of New Year's was unrivaled by any other occasion.

We were a group of fourteen- and fifteen-year-olds. I was at the age where I only needed to check in with my family before rushing out the door with my posse. Together in our independence, we took the town center first. We were a roving pack, eight or ten of us, joined at times by more school friends, and then left to ourselves again. I stayed closest to Isaac and his girlfriend, and Sabrina, my friend who was a girl. We had hamburgers and cups of fruit doused with lemon and chile powder. We spilled Isaac's sister's pork skins—the big girl didn't need them anyway—before we dashed off in a cloud of hysteria. We stood and watched the fireworks at midnight as people all around us stared at the splendor in the sky. And then we strolled the maze of streets, greeting friends with New Year hugs and procuring homemade treats from the spreads on tables in open homes.

After two in the morning or so, Isaac nudged my elbow as he told his girlfriend, "You ought to go home. Your parents will be worried."

I looked down at a plastic bag he carried, unsure from where he had gotten it, and I could tell that its contents were heavy. As the girls discussed their plans, Isaac opened the bag for me to see the pair of *caguamas*, liter-sized bottles of beer. I hated the taste of beer.

"They can come with us," I whispered to him.

"No. It's not enough for four. Shh."

I decided to follow his lead. I had no reason to oppose his wanting to be alone with me. The girls went off then, with a final hug.

"She was bothering me," Isaac explained. "Bad breath. Her hands get all sweaty too." He crunched up his nose. "Come on, let's go find some place to drink these."

We hiked up into one of the hills, where people used to say the souls of the mummies drifted between the canyons. Not many kids dared to go up there in the nighttime. Isaac apparently had. He took me directly to a perch, a sort of ledge formed by the flat surface of a stone boulder from where we could see the lights of the town center and hear an occasional burst or pop of firecrackers. He took out the *caguamas*, pried off their lids with his teeth, and handed me a lukewarm behemoth. They weren't named after giant sea turtles for nothing.

My hands and ears started to sting with the December air, colder at this altitude than down in the streets. "It's getting pretty late, and cold. Don't you think we should head back?" I said.

"Shut up, 'Turo," he answered, so I did.

He set down his bottle and lay back on the rock. I watched him, and took the length of his body in. He closed his eyes, and my heart nearly stopped when he started rubbing himself.

"I feel kinda horny, don't you?"

"I don't know," I said. No one had ever asked me that. I hadn't ever seen another guy touch himself like I did when I got the chance.

"It's that my girlfriend doesn't want to. You know?"

"Oh." I nodded with feigned empathy.

"Is anyone around?"

I surveyed the hillside around us, hardly sure how we even got there in the darkness. "No. Nobody."

"Don't say anything, alright?" He pulled it out and started masturbating right there. Then he coaxed me to touch it and jerk it for him, before the goo came out. Afterward, he made me do the same— pull it out and let him yank it until my goo came out too. He'd know I wouldn't say anything, he said, if we both did the same thing.

Just between friends, he clarified, a little help, like treating for taco or loaning a soccer ball. Of course, I shrugged, like no big deal. So I never mentioned it again, or the other few times we repeated it. Then Isaac got a different girl who did want to do it. She got pregnant a year later, so they got married, and I, instead of finding a girl like the rest of my friends did, kept my feelers out for another Isaac. I wondered what Mamá would say if she knew, or the padre, if I confessed. She might hate me, I thought, for the terrible sin. But I couldn't help it. I knew somehow I had to be with a man.

Ay, amor. I had no idea it would be you. I could never have imagined the road my life would take. Or how the confessions and crepe paper celebrations would lead me there. I suffered, at times, like you. I felt the fear that my family might reject me, or that I'd be banished from my town. Sometimes I walked through the thickest of fogs, wondering what I might hit, or if I might suddenly fall in some hole and be swallowed by the earth. Leaving of my free will made all the difference.

Isaac's sister cornered me one day after school started up again in January. She pushed me against the jagged wall of the drugstore. "What'd you do to my brother?" she demanded. Her forearm weighed heavily against my chest. I figured she was still mad about the pork skins.

"What are you talking about?"

"His girlfriend told me you and he went to the Alley of the Kiss together."

"We didn't. Shut up." I was too old to play such childish games. And she was supposedly almost a woman, too, a hefty, bitter woman with crooked teeth.

"Maybe we'll see what everyone else thinks about it."

"Don't be stupid," I said, fearing she might spread rumors, fearing the truth of them, and fearing what they all would say if they found out.

I stayed away from Isaac's sister and felt a wave of relief when she left for Nuevo León to study, never having spread the rumors... that I knew of.

FIFTEEN

CHAVA had been working on the crepe paper for a few days, and things at the restaurant returned to normal, except for an occasional harassing phone call. The wait staff became accustomed to them and readily hung the phone up. Chava had officially moved into Joe's home under an agreement to keep home stuff at home, and work stuff at work, and to let Joe know if he wouldn't be home for some reason. Chava would pay a nominal rent until he could get his finances caught up, the details of which were "strictly personal."

Joe reflected as he flipped the Señor Septiembre kitchen calendar page over to Señor Octubre, a dark-skinned delight in white mesh underwear. For the most part, he enjoyed having someone else in the house. It gave him more reason to actually have food there and to maintain a decent level of cleanliness and orderliness. The mere thought of Chava poking his head into Joe's room obliged him to make the bed, for instance. Additionally, he appreciated Chava's assistance with the *ofrenda*. The task of putting it together was a simple one, but sharing it with someone who had meant so much to Arturo increased its significance.

Over the past week or two, Joe and Chava had formed the habit of walking home from the restaurant together. Tonight they carried terracotta dishes from the restaurant for the *ofrenda*, a couple cans of jalapeño-stuffed olives from Mercado Gómez, and tall candles in glass vases. As he walked, Joe imagined himself years later, as he sometimes did—an old man in an old flat, putting up the *ofrenda*, longing for his love. He wasn't sure if the ritual helped him by making the sorrow concrete, or if it only perpetuated the pain and stalled the healing.

Would he ever be done with it? Would there be a time when he no longer needed it? Arturo hadn't ceased the practice for his grandparents and he hadn't seemed to wallow in pain.

Of course, esteem for one's grandparents differed from the lingering loss of a partner. In a way, grandparents were "supposed" to die—people expected their grandparents to predecease them. A partner, on the other hand, had no such presupposition. Some closure, at least, would have helped. There was never a body—Joe cringed at the thought—no funeral, no memorial service. Only a final phone call from the other side of the border, and his last words: "I'll be there in two or tree days. I love you. I'll see you in a few days. I won't say good-bye, then, but *hasta luego*." Until later.

Those days afterward had been filled with anguish. The phone calls, the trip south, and the unanswered questions. Empty months followed, until one day he finally pronounced the words, "He's dead." They fell like a lead weight, its heavy thud reverberating through him. He'd become dizzy when he said it. He'd been standing in the middle of the restaurant and had to sit down. No other explanation existed. Arturo had died.

He looked over at Chava who walked up the sidewalk with his characteristic energetic bounce, both hoodish and queeny at the same time. He'd been in a pleasant mood these past few days, a mood that had rubbed off onto Joe and brought life to the house.

Hands full in the darkness, Joe fumbled for the keys. Chava stood beside him, stepped closer to the door, and from beneath his feet came the distinctive sound of broken glass. They looked at each other. Chava set his bag down to similar crunches. He reached into the pocket of his baggy pants and pulled out a stainless steel knife, unfolding it without the showy flair he'd mentioned when describing the incident in the Tenderloin.

Joe's heart raced. He jabbed at the doorknob with his key, shaking loose another shard of glass that fell to the porch, crashing with the others.

"Fuckin' pussies," Chava said as Joe finally opened the door and flicked on the porch light.

"It looks like they didn't break in," Joe said, noticing a hole about the size of a basketball, well within reach of the door lock. "They wouldn't have locked the door."

He opened the door. At the base of the stairs he spotted the culprit, a white, irregularly shaped chunk of concrete about the size of a brick.

Joe looked at Chava who read his mind. "I don't think it was Dario. He's all talk."

"Who else would it be, Chava?"

Chava only shrugged.

"Don't worry. I'll pay for it. But you better find out if Dario had anything to do with this."

"Okay. I'll find out. This ain't over."

"Now, put your knife away. We don't want anyone to get killed over this. It's a piece of glass."

"It's territory, man."

"Chava," Joe said as he put his hand on the young man's forearm, "it's a piece of glass. Get the broom. We'll have it fixed tomorrow morning. And in the meantime, we have an *ofrenda* to set up."

Joe went upstairs and started moving some furniture to make space for the *ofrenda*. He pulled the serape from the wall and placed it over a card table like a tablecloth. He began to arrange the items he'd brought and then decided he'd start with a picture. He wanted to use a different one this year, so he went to his room to find one in the closet.

Chava came up the stairs with a dustpan full of broken glass in one hand and the concrete block in the other. He passed Joe with a guilty expression on his face. "I have to make a phone call," he said. He found the phone and went into his bedroom with it, closing the door behind him.

Fifteen minutes later, Joe returned to the *ofrenda* with a picture of Arturo and himself at Mirror Lake in Yosemite. Shortly before opening the restaurant, they'd taken a trip there, and after a long hike admired the pristine view. Arturo had stared in awe, as if hypnotized by the crystal reflection of Half Dome and North Dome on the still surface of the lake. The picture somehow captured the elation and accomplishment on their tired, sweaty faces, as well as the blue sleeve of Arturo's extended arm. He always loved taking pictures of himself.

Joe tried to be respectful of Chava's private phone conversation. But having placed the *ofrenda* so close to the bedroom door, he found it hard not to hear the heated conversation. Many of the words were muffled, fast-spoken Spanish Joe could hardly decipher. A few stood out, though.

"I told you I can't give you any more money right now!"

Joe felt guilty, as if he were spying. Still, he was as interested in a solution to this feud as Chava was, and he hoped this was a step in the right direction. At least Chava was confronting the issue in a semi-peaceful manner.

"No, I'm not going over there! I'm not doing it!"

Joe could only imagine the other side of the conversation. A moment later, Chava came out of the bedroom. Joe put on a pleasant, innocent face. "Everything okay?" he asked.

"Don't worry about it."

"I just want to know things will be settled."

"I'll take care of it, I said."

"Fine. Then come help me with this."

To Joe, the beauty of the *ofrenda* was its thoughtfulness—they'd make additions one by one over the next couple weeks as memories begot corresponding symbolic pieces. Chava's mood changed from the hostility of his phone conversation to reverence for their departed friend. He popped the lid from one of the cans of olives and filled a terracotta dish. After lighting the first candle, they each grabbed an olive, touched them together as with wine glasses, and said in unison, "To Arturo." Just when Joe was about to say good night, Chava told him to wait a second. He returned with an item in his hand, which he placed on the table.

"What is it?" Joe asked.

"A memory," Chava said.

Joe looked at the plastic toy. "A motorcycle?" He would have never connected a motorcycle with Arturo.

"Yeah. I don't know why I didn't think of it before."

"Why a motorcycle?"

"For our trips out. He never told you, did he?"

"What now? Was he a Hell's Angel or something?"

"No. But he used to take me on rides around the city. He told me not to tell you we went on a motorcycle that one of my friends let us borrow."

"I knew you used to hang out sometimes. Your 'private times'—mother and daughter—but he never said anything about a bike."

"He probably thought you'd get mad. He had no license, no insurance, and 'motorcycles are dangerous.' They're fun too. I felt like a real biker chick."

"Where'd you go?"

"All over the city—Fisherman's Wharf, North Beach, Highway 1—gliding up and down the hills. We had a blast. One time we went all the way down to Pacifica and through the hills to Devil's Slide. He was probably right—you would have killed him. Haven't you ever been on one?"

"I hate them. One of my uncles got killed on one."

"See. 'Turo was right about you. He liked it, though. He said he felt free in the open air."

"Hmmm. I guess there's always something you don't know about people."

"Too late to get mad now, dog."

"I know," Joe said, laughing. "I'm just a little surprised—you think you know everything about a person, about your own partner, and here he kept your secret from me for all that time. Motorcycle... I had no idea. Now, how about those crepe paper cutouts?"

"Patience, José, I still got lots of time."

SIXTEEN

THE Arizona desert reached over 110 degrees. People sought shelter from the blistering sun in their air-conditioned rooms. The people in the houses we worked at, that is, and sometimes they'd peer out the front or back windows, watching as we dug the canals for their irrigation systems. With my oversized sombrero, I felt like a *campesino* from a César Chávez labor movement poster as I toiled in the fields. Hardly agriculture, these were the gardens of upscale Arizona houses, gardens the gabachos would drive past as they pulled their cars into driveways and stepped into their refrigerated homes. It was as if they were making a sightseeing tour, the gardens symbols of their accomplishments, ones they would never lay their own hands on. We dug up the soil, we installed the automatic watering systems, and then we maintained the gardens for a fixed monthly fee. They looked at the gardens from behind car windows and living room curtains.

The boss was a longtime immigrant from Coahuila. He'd been in the United States for three decades or more and had mastered English better than any of us. He had the connections, he had the Nextel radio and the fancy sunglasses, and he'd stop by each of his work sites two or three times a day to check on progress.

One day, the sun really punished us, and the air stood as still as the red Arizona rock formations. We'd spent two full days on the spacious front yard of a southwestern mansion, my roommates and I digging the ditches with narrow shovels and two-handed picks. We spent about as much time at the water cooler as in the soil to avoid heat stroke, and my skin was as dark as a Cuban's. Something didn't seem right about the job, though, and I recalled a lesson from one of my architecture courses on landscaping and plumbing. I had taken a few crude measurements by stepping the length of the ditches, and I judged the slope with my thumb in the air, a closed eye, and my tongue sticking out.

When the boss drove by for his inspection, I told him the pipes were too wide. They wouldn't provide the water pressure for the type of irrigation heads we were going to install. He looked at me, like, what did I know? I was nothing but a stupid ditchdigger who had just crossed the border. I'm sure he figured I was as uneducated as the rest, who actually weren't uneducated at all.

He looked at me as I talked. As if I hadn't spoken a word, he clapped his hands, stomped the heel of his pointy brown boot down to smudge out a cigarette he'd thrown on the ground, and told us to hurry up and finish. He got back into his truck and drove off.

The next day, the PVC pipe installed and buried, we opened the water valve. The pop-up heads didn't. They struggled to come out of their holes. Instead of young, perky prairie dogs, we had a row of convalescent banana slugs. Water drizzled out at each of the heads, leaving a wet spot like the crotch of a scared boy. I pulled off my sombrero and held it with both hands at my waist, knowing that "I told you so" would be perfectly correct yet totally inappropriate. Macho men from Coahuila didn't like to be wrong, even if they hadn't been in Coahuila for half a century.

Of course, the boss man came to check it out and angrily sucked on his cigarette. He looked up at the sun, as if judging the time of day, and told us to dig it up and replace the pipes with thinner ones. He didn't have the gonads to as much as look at me. I didn't know my blood could actually get any closer to boiling. Worse, we didn't get paid for the extra day it took. On the contrary, he said we were lucky to get paid the same since we had lost money on extra parts. And anyway, we got paid by project, not by time.

I didn't know what to do with myself. Once inside the apartment, I paced the hallway, until Rafael, one of the roommates, threw his keys at me, telling me to take his bike for a spin and get some air. I had ridden a little 50cc bike back home, and knew how to shift motorcycle gears and work the hand clutch and footbrake. I took him up on it.

From that day on, I frequently borrowed his motorcycle. Nothing like that 50cc trinket, this one was a Yamaha Seca 550. I'd don a scuffed helmet and leave the world behind. It gave me lots of time to think, and I entertained myself by singing aloud the only line of the Lynyrd Skynyrd medley I knew: *I'm as free as a birt now, and this birt will never shange.* True, it was like flying, and the Arizona deserts offered hundreds of miles on which to get airborne.

Around the December holidays, the hot desert weather changed in just a few days to near freezing. I didn't care—I still needed to get out and fly. Wishing I could open my wings and fly home for a while, I took the I-19 one night, almost a two-hundred-mile straight shot down toward Nogales, flying like a free bird. Until I ran out of gas. The free bird became a desert tortoise pushing the bike on a two-lane, unlit road somewhere in the desert. I hadn't seen any establishments for miles, and I cursed the gaugeless gas tank. I must have been close to the border; I'd been driving for two hours.

The night wore on and I grew too tired to push anymore. I considered dropping the bike and leaving it there, but knew I'd have no way of paying for it if and when I made it back to Phoenix. I propped it up in the sand off the road, concerned a car might come by, its driver not paying much attention, and run it over and me as well. I leaned against the bike, hugged myself in my leather jacket for warmth, and fell asleep. I'd considered the possibility that I'd die in my sleep and never wake up.

"Partner. Partner." A man's voice, and his flashlight, woke me. He put his hand on my shoulder. "Are you okay?" Groggy, I recognized the forest green of his border-patrol uniform and could see his red cheeks and strawberry-blond hair in the reflection of his light. His white teeth seemed to jump out of the darkness. He got me up and sat me on the seat of the motorcycle, patting my shoulder.

"Have some water," he said, handing me a full bottle. It went down my throat cold, and it stirred my insides and snapped me out of my stupor. I saw the truck he drove, a white SUV with a cage in the back, and I knew I'd be in there pretty soon, once I regained my bearings. The tags on the bike were expired, I carried no license, and I had no ID.

"Yo tenía una de esas," he said in a terrible Texan accent. I had one of those, he was trying to say, a Yamaha Seca. He told me it was his first vehicle when he was sixteen.

He walked to the back of the SUV and opened the gate. I got up from the motorcycle seat, knowing the time had come for me to crawl into his truck and become his prisoner. He had a gun, and I had no motivation to run. I walked toward the back, grateful, actually, for his pleasant treatment of me.

Then he pulled a heavy red tank from his truck and looked at me. "Gas?" he asked. "You need gas, right?"

"Yes."

He asked me for the key and filled up the tank of the Yamaha. The bikes were called "cold starts" for a reason. We hit the ignition switch until the battery died. There was no other way than to push-start it, so he helped me get it back on the road and he worked up a sweat pushing me down the empty highway until I could get it started. I thought of just driving off—he'd never catch me at a hundred miles per hour. I didn't, though. I put the kickstand down and walked back with him to the truck, still thinking he might have to take me in. Instead, he gave me a bottle of water for the road and told me in awful Spanish that the worst mistake people out in the desert made was not carrying enough water. He shook my hand. I couldn't help myself, so I gave him a hug, still wondering why I hadn't heard the click of handcuffs and the radio call for backup.

I understood there were things about people beyond what one assumes. I thought the Coahuila boss would have respected me. I thought the gabacho border patrolman would arrest me. I had come to realize there were many things I thought about people that were wrong, and parts of each individual that I would have never guessed existed inside them. There is more inside you too, amor, that you still don't know.

SEVENTEEN

THIS time the restaurant had been hit—graffiti scrawled across the storefront from one side to the other in black, gang-style letters. The ghetto glyphs were unintelligible to Joe, symbols of the underworld. He stood outside with paint cans and brushes, scrapers and scrubbers. And this time, Joe had called the cops, knowing they wouldn't do much about it but hoping their presence might somehow ward off any future attacks. He waited for Chava to come in for his shift. Unsure what Chava could do about it, Joe only knew things were getting worse instead of better.

He had his eye out down the busy block for either the police or Chava to show up. He spotted someone unexpected. Even a block away, Alberto couldn't be missed in his green and yellow sweats, as big as a hot-air balloon. Joe put the tools down on the sidewalk and held his hands out wide to hug the man who had finally returned.

The big man sported a wide grin. His face was drenched with sweat, enough to make Joe reconsider the embrace. Too late—the big walrus had Joe wrapped in his arms. "You're a sight for sore eyes," Joe said. "Come on in and have some breakfast."

Alberto looked at the damage left indiscriminately across the building, as if a paint-wielding tornado had passed. "No thanks," he said. "I'm actually on my way to work."

"Oh?"

"Yes. I've decided to start walking."

"Good for you."

"New motif?" Alberto asked.

"Yeah. We thought we'd go punk for awhile."

"I see. Maybe some nice bags of garbage out here would help, or an old car seat people could sit on."

Sobering up, Joe said, "I'm waiting for Chava to get here. He's got to put an end to this."

"Ah." The big man's eyes widened. "Speak of the devil."

Joe turned around to see the effeminate thug walking their way.

"I better let you go," Alberto said. "I will be here for lunch today." He leaned in to Joe's ear. "Limits, Joe. Set the limits." And then he headed up the street toward Chava, looking like the entire Brazilian soccer team taking on the Mission District all at once.

Joe watched as Chava gave Alberto a nod. A second later, Chava turned and looked at the restaurant, surveying the damage. "What the fuck?" he said.

"You tell me, Chava."

Chava shrugged. "Man, I don't know."

Joe put his hands on his hips. "How much do you owe him, anyway?"

"It's not what you think, okay? There's no way this could have been Dario. He don't do this kind of shit. He ain't no tagger."

"Say what you like. This time I called the cops."

"You did?"

"I gave you a chance to put an end to it. First the house door, now this. It's gone too far."

"Suit yourself. I'm telling you, he couldn't have done this." He pointed at other buildings on the block with graffiti on their walls. "Look where you are, man. You think he did that and that and that one over there?"

"Just too much coincidence. I don't believe in coincidence."

"Whatever you say. I say Dario's a pussy. And I mean to take care of him for once and for all."

"We'll see what the police have to say."

"Yeah, real crime-stoppers." Chava sarcastically fluttered his ten fingers like a spook. "All you need to do is let the gangstas know you don't want them marking your territory. You think the cops'll get them before they make a Picasso out of this shit?"

"You tried your way, now I'll try mine."

"Okay, boss. I'm goin' in. Don't want to be late."

An hour later, a policewoman scolded a jammed digital camera. "I said camera mode!" She pushed the same button over and over until it finally beeped. "Okay," she told Joe, "step aside so I can get this. I haven't seen this sign before. Could be a new kid in town."

"Ever heard of a guy named Dario?"

She lowered the camera for a second to think. "No. Mario, but no Dario. You got an address or a number?"

"Down by Market Street, I think."

"Hmm... they usually tag their own neighborhoods. They don't want to be getting up in other people's places unless they want some trouble."

"Couldn't it be a personal vendetta?"

"I guess. Did you cross somebody?"

"No. Not exactly. I mean, maybe he thinks I did but I don't think so."

"I'll put his name in the report. We'll see if anything pops up. If you find any solid evidence, let me know." She handed him a business card.

"Thank you, Officer." He pointed at the entrance. "You want to come in, maybe have a doughnut?" It slipped out. He immediately wished he could take it back.

"Very funny, sir," she said, tucking the camera in its pouch. "I don't do doughnuts. But do you have any of that Mexican sweet bread?"

LATER in the afternoon, Alberto came in as promised for lunch. "We've missed you," Joe said to him.

"It's been weird not coming in. After cleaning your floor with my back, I thought about not coming back."

"I don't blame you."

"But in a way, you know, like Oprah said—the universe sends you messages, do you listen to them?"

"You heard a message?"

"I didn't have to strain very hard. It's stupid, I know. Do you think I don't see myself every day in the mirror? People snicker at me, sometimes behind my back and sometimes not. Even you've told me things I didn't want to hear. Hey, Oprah had her robust days too. Maybe those punks weren't entirely wrong. I mean, things had to go that far before I would listen."

"I'm sorry about that. I feel like I should have done something."

"No. Don't be sorry. I've been doling out advice for years. I wouldn't take any, though, until that one, Chainsaw, kicked some sense into me... literally. Now, if Oprah could do it, I can too. It's time to bite the bullet—the nonfat bullet. Anyway, you don't need always to second-guess yourself. You did what you thought was right in the moment. Sometimes people just have to go off and grow by themselves."

Joe held up his order tablet, almost afraid to ask. "So, will it be the usual?" he said between clenched teeth.

"Yeah, double portion... of your best green salad. Low-fat dressing please."

Joe smiled like a proud father. "Coming right up, my friend."

EIGHTEEN

AMOR, there were many things I never told you. Good thing. Worse than getting angry, you probably would have been hurt, or found a way to make it all your fault. You might have called it all off for my sake. Some people believe in 100 percent honesty between partners. They demonize the omissions too. Some of those same people probably believe in torture and cruelty as a way to get things done. No, there are certain things a partner goes through by himself, obstacles that, once overcome, bring him back to the relationship stronger, more stable, and more ready to contribute his part. I didn't tell you all because I shouldn't have.

You saved us by opening the restaurant. Long before that, when I had only been in San Francisco with you for a year, I would get up from bed some nights and leave you in the bedroom alone. You slept so peacefully, like a child, your still eyelashes, darker than your blond hair, making your eyes look like those of a doll, the kind that closes its eyes when it's laid down. Sometimes I would start thinking about stuff and couldn't fall asleep, so I'd sit in the living room, prop my feet up on the couch, and stare at the wall with a bottle of Corralejo and a shot glass.

I had become a laborer again, albeit a restaurant laborer, after having sworn to myself not to. I had left Phoenix with such a foul taste in my mouth. Sure, I had earned dollars, saved a little and sent some home. I'd also learned why so many Mexicans stayed for such a short while and then went home in spite of facing unemployment again. Money isn't everything. And the American dream is exactly that—a dream—and everyone should know dreams aren't reality.

Where was the liberty in the land of the free when everything was governed by the clock and by money? When I rode the bus, I'd watch the way the people around me inside the bus or in their cars or on the sidewalk depended on their cell phones like appendages. If they weren't making phone calls to the baby sitter or the bank, they were checking the time because, undoubtedly, they were running late. You'd think with all the running, they would have been trimmer. The stores and banks would give credit to anyone, even us illegals who had no licenses or Social Security numbers to prove we existed. But to the banks and stores and used car lots, we existed. So they gave us credit, all on easy-payment plans, and then we started running to pay those plans. Then we started running to drive-through fast-food restaurants, and the quick-check lines in the supermarkets. I had started running on the motorcycle, but instead of running in the pack like the race where all the cars go around and around in the same circle to see who outlasts everybody else, I guess my running was more cross-country.

In San Francisco, I ran a little on the motorcycle with Chava. I never told you. And the not telling you enhanced the freedom of it, ignoring you and your gringo rules, your licenses and full stops before the limit lines. Chava took away a bit from the freedom. He held onto me tightly, yelled all the time in my ear, nasty comments about people on the road. Besides, he couldn't always get the motorcycle, so my running started to take the form of the shot glass and the big blue bottle of tequila. And Chuy and Chepa.

I had hit such a patch of depression. You didn't see it much because you didn't see me much, and that was part of what caused the depression in the first place. I had bought into the need to work, to enter the race again, and run for you. I felt like a dog doing tricks for a treat.

In truth, I missed home more than I ever told you. I wanted to walk up the haunted hill in the darkness and look down on the lights of Guanajuato. I wanted to return home and see Mamá. I wanted the raucousness of the Festival Cervantino and the unity of New Year's. I even wanted to see the mummies again, stare into their blank eyes and peer into their open mouths and wonder what their names were, what had killed them, and what they were feeling in that moment. Even escaping on the motorcycle with Chava to the highest peaks of the city, I found street lights where I wanted darkness, and carefully painted lines in the streets, no-parking signs, and speed limits. Limits, limits, everything was limited!

Chuy and Chepa started to invite me out. Their rebelliousness at work attracted me. They'd mock the boss the second he turned his back. They'd come in drunk and leave with stolen meat and cheese. They'd overly spice the food of the gabachos just to watch them choke and cough, and they'd flirt with the cute busboys and try to entice them into the walk-in refrigerator.

They enticed me too, with flight. "Let's get the fuck out of here," one of them would say after a tiring night shift. "Let's show this town what a party is!"

I told them no at first. And then came November 11, the day of my saint, San Martín. You didn't even know my second name, did you? Halloween and the Day of the Dead had just passed. You had been partied out and had as much Mexican tradition as you could take for a while. It was a Wednesday, you had to work the next day, and so I assumed I'd pass the day with no cake and no presents. I wasn't in the bosom of Guanajuato, after all, and you couldn't have known that in the absence of a San Arturo, my family always celebrated the Day of San Martín for me.

Chuy and Chepa didn't know it was my saint's day either. To them it was just Wednesday night at Esta Noche, and a very special Wednesday, too, because Nacho Mama was scheduled to perform, and they loved that nasty drag queen from Sinaloa. "Come on. Don't be such a party pooper." For a second, I had suspected they knew it was my party day. They didn't, but I finally gave in and made my own party out of it.

Nacho Mama was hilarious, and Chuy and Chepa got me dragged up to the stage, not to celebrate my saint's day, but because I was a virgin to her show. They poured cheap tequila down my throat before Nacho Mama dry-humped me in the missionary position. I could tell Nacho Mama was actually a big daddy down there when she rubbed her coochie up against mine, and actually, along with the tequila and pitchers of beer, it got me a little turned on.

The show ended and the bar closed down, but our private party went on. Chuy suggested we all go to his place, where he had some fresh pot from Mazatlán. I hadn't smoked much pot before and I was in the mood to try anything, so we all sucked on his very cliché dick-shaped pipe. Chepa started deep-throating it and doing his sexy dance on the coffee table.

Before I knew it, Chepa had his gyrating crotch in my face. He was a short guy with a bit of a paunch for his age, early twenties. He was nothing I would have ever considered sexy. Then Chuy leaned over and pulled Chepa's zipper down, his bulge instantly adding four or five points to his sexiness rating. Chuy followed that up by pulling Chepa's pants and underwear all the way down in one fell swoop. Myself, I would have died. I would have yanked them up in an instant and run for the door. Perhaps the pot and liquor changed things a bit—he kept on gyrating. He put it in my face and I could smell his musky aroma, which got me undeniably horny.

He brought it closer to my face. I licked my lips, readying my mouth. But then Chuy got up on the couch, shaky and awkward on his knees, and did what I was about to do. I hadn't thought they ever messed around together, and I suspected the stupefying substances had something to do with it. He gave his best shot at taking the whole thing in his mouth. A second later, Chepa pulled it out of Chuy's mouth, followed immediately by the contents of Chuy's stomach. He barfed all over Chepa's groin and legs and the underwear bunched down at his ankles. The scene was sobering.

I thought of you at home. I had never cheated on you. I had promised not to. Of course, lately you and I hadn't had much sex. I think neither of us had wanted it for a while. But I knew if and when I did that, I had the person at home to do it with. I gathered the pieces of my dignity and faithfulness that I could, thanked God for Chepa's vomit, and staggered down the many flights of stairs of Chuy's apartment building and out onto the sidewalk and into the crisp air of November.

I wasn't sure where I was, but somehow I made it home. I felt like I had been walking a precipice and had nearly jumped into the abyss. Then I realized I wanted the solid ground. I guess that was my present for the day of my saint—to know I had something worthwhile and I wanted to keep it. I had you.

Things didn't change right away. I stayed at that restaurant awhile in those shifts that conflicted with yours. I went out with Chuy and Chepa again. I had too much to drink too many times. But I never got close to either Chuy or Chepa's crotch again. I was never even tempted again. I didn't say anything to either of them. For all I knew, they hadn't remembered any of it. I could only imagine Chuy waking up with his pants down, encrusted with chunks of red regurgitation. I had a personal learning experience—I surpassed an obstacle, and set my own limit. I had made a promise to you then, in my own mind, and I thought that was where it best belonged, inside me.

Drinking with Chuy and Chepa could have led me astray in many different ways. You saved us by deciding to open the restaurant. You knew me, in some ways better than I knew myself, and you knew I needed something more. Perhaps you didn't even realize it at the time, but sometimes we know things without knowing we know them. You knew we had love worth salvaging, worth risking so much for. You knew it was there, you knew we loved each other, and that it was on the brink of slipping away. Yes, you saved us. God, love is beautiful.

NINETEEN

AS CHAVA had predicted, the police did nothing about the graffiti. The officer had taken her sweet bread and never returned. Joe had taped her business card on the podium, but later decided to put it in a drawer in his desk at home, where it would inevitably be consumed by the paper-eating monster that lived there.

One night in late October, Joe had prepared tostadas with the beef pulled and shredded the way Arturo had showed him. He topped it with freshly made salsa from the restaurant, and thin slices of tomatoes and radishes. To drink, he uncorked a bottle of pinot noir from Napa Valley, one Arturo happened to enjoy. The dinner was a testament to the cultural mix the couple had achieved. He set the table for two, lit a candle, and walked over to knock on Chava's door.

"I'm tired of putting up with this." Joe began listening in on another heated phone call. He thought better of knocking, putting aside the hope he'd had for a sort of family dinner.

"Money, money! You always ask for money!"

Joe wondered how much of his relationship with Dario Chava had failed to mention. It all sounded insidious. After all this time, the two were still speaking, yet there never seemed to be any peace. He suspected Chava went to visit him on some of his many nights out, probably a classic love-hate relationship, both long-lasting and rotten. He felt pity for Chava, whose self-esteem must have been low to put up with that.

"No! I'm not going with you!"

Joe backed away from the door and went to sit by himself in the kitchen. He heard a few more angry words from Chava's bedroom before the talking stopped again. Chava's door opened and the kid dashed by in a flash. Joe heard Chava's footsteps as he bolted down the stairs. The front door opened and shut. Would he make a straight line to Dario's house? Joe imagined the two, passionate, perhaps, screaming at each other, maybe hitting each other, before steamy sex with pounding, punishing thrusts. At least there hadn't been another block thrown through the window.

Joe glanced over at Arturo's *ofrenda*. The candle was lit, the tiny flame flickering near the bottom of the vase, the dim halo of Virgin Mary shifting between amber and brown. Joe would have to change the candle soon. The motorcycle stood beside the candle, resting on its tiny plastic kickstand. Joe could picture Arturo beside it, holding his helmet under his arm and giving Joe a satisfied grin for having conquered the city, sped through traffic, and lost himself before coming home to Joe. Arturo the Hell's Angel. Incredible. Kind of hot in a James Dean sort of way.

Without a word, Chava had hung the crepe paper on the wall to make a shroud around the *ofrenda*. One of Chava's hidden talents—the kid could make cutouts from the most fragile paper. He'd sit for hours with tiny, pointy scissors and an idea in his head. Sometime later, he'd have a work of art. This year's butterflies were large ones, each made from an entire sheet of paper. The veins of the wings were paper, while the orange of the monarchs had been cut away. He'd made a dozen or so, each similar to the others but distinct, and each butterfly in midflight, headed south for Mexico.

Joe thought of Arturo as one of those butterflies, flying home and finally free. He had always been so sentimental, a real mama's boy, and Joe had guessed that on many occasions he had flown home, if only in his mind, to the hills of Guanajuato, where life seemed simpler. There had always been unfairness in their relationship, and inequity, a reflection of the same unfairness and inequity in the world. Americans had all the money. Money ruled. Americans could go wherever they pleased. Gays couldn't get married. Yet every relationship suffered some sacrifice or inequity.

Perhaps something in Chava told him the suffering with Dario made it worth more. Perhaps he thought Dario was the only one that could care for him or want him. He probably felt worthless—without family and without a real home. Joe and Arturo at times had tried to be a replacement, a new family and a new home. It was up to Chava to accept it, though. Joe took the crepe paper in again, and the beauty that came from the mind and hands of this lost boy. He was full of surprises, no doubt. After all, Arturo's motorcycle riding had surprised him. Doubtless there existed more aspects of Chava than Joe had ever known. And who was he to judge? At Chava's age, Joe had grappled with a relationship as well.

Joe had been brought up in a small, run-down neighborhood in Boise, where he and the local kids had played tennis on cracked concrete courts with metal nets. From a trunk in his basement, one of the kids had dug up wooden rackets with the strings intact, and they prolonged the life of worn-out tennis balls by fluffing up the felt with sandpaper and scouring pads. Church on Wednesdays and Sundays, casseroles on Tuesdays, Friday garbage days, and Saturdays for mowing the clumpy lawn. The most exciting part of Joe's childhood was inviting a friend to their Fourth of July barbecues for mustard-and-ketchup hotdogs and a garden hose Slip 'N Slide.

Joe had graduated high school in 1993 not far from the top of his class and received a Pell Grant for the ISU outreach program in Boise. A detestable secret churned inside him, one that would certainly earn the disdain of the church and the ire of his family. The era of AIDS had begun, and the preacher's told-you-so sermon affirmed the due punishment for the sodomites. Still, like so many young gay men of that time, one way or another, Joe had to go figure out the churning inside him.

He had no gay friends and had never been to any gay establishment. One June, shortly after his eighteenth birthday, he came across a short article near the end of the local section of the *Idaho Press-Tribune*: "Gay Organizers Seek Support." The first few paragraphs discussed a bar owner and a few of his comrades who were considering starting a local chapter of ACT UP. The next paragraph reported their neighbors' concerns and complaints. And the closing sentence mentioned the city's first "pride" event that would take place at the aptly named "Sin," one of two gay bars in Boise. After reading the article and committing the date to memory, he closed the paper, feeling as guilty as a thief, and set it unassumingly in its place on the living room end table.

He would take a big risk in going, but he had a compulsion inside him, greater than simple curiosity. After mowing the lawn, he made up an excuse. Movies, a plausible lie, and pizza with a friend, not one from their church, but who went to another acceptable church nonetheless. With the drinking age at twenty-one, Joe wasn't quite sure why he wanted to go to Sin, but the temptation was too great. He wouldn't forgive himself later if he didn't go.

Once on the bus, he kept his eyes open like an undercover agent as he traveled across town, on the lookout for schoolmates, neighbors, or parishioners of his church. He walked a couple blocks from the bus stop toward Sin, uncertain what to expect, but expecting something. His heart beat fast before he turned the final corner. Would there be a gleeful crowd outside, a riotous mob, reporters, motorcycles, or even Gloria Gaynor in the flesh? There was nothing. The place stood there like an empty house with a closed door. A neon beer sign was on in the window, and the sign above the door read "SI." Had he mistaken the date? He stood across the street until someone finally walked in.

"Are you coming?" a guy said from beside Joe. He was a good-looking, manly Idahoan at least ten years older than Joe. The guy seemed to have appeared from nowhere.

"Umm...." He felt caught. "Yeah, I guess. I just... I'm not twenty-one."

"Come on. Walk in with me. I know the owner. He won't say anything. I'm Clif, by the way, not pronounced like Cliff but Clif, like 'life'."

"Okay. Joe."

One hour and two beers later, in the midst of a small group of proud middle-aged homosexuals, Joe kissed a man—Clif—for the first time. In that moment, he confirmed to himself that he was gay. And he thought he was in love. After years of internal struggle, it seemed far too easy to be true.

TWENTY

I DID long for Guanajuato and resent, at times, not being able to go there. When I had returned from Phoenix, I was sure I'd never leave home again. The summer heat, the winter cold, the backbreaking work, and the underclass status of an illegal were enough to keep me from Arizona forever, not to mention the scapegoating of the aliens for all political and economic woes. They could keep the Grand Canyon, and I would be happy enough in the humble hills and valleys back home.

San Francisco was another story. A true hodgepodge—all types of Latinos and blacks, Asians and whites, Catholics, Christians, Jews, Buddhists, Muslims, men, women, manly girls, girly men, bikers, thrashers, punks, crazies, lazies, junkies, yuppies, gays, dykes, and everything in between—all within some forty square miles. I thought at times I could walk around with blue skin and three orange eyes and nobody would look twice.

I'd had a pair of clip-on skates when I was a kid, something one of my uncles found in a box of his. Within five minutes back then I learned that skates and cobblestones were a bad mix. The inline skates you gave me for my birthday my first year with you looked like futuristic gizmos compared to the clunky metal things I'd had as a child. And the broad, smooth asphalt on the main boulevard through Golden Gate Park made a better training spot than anything back home, especially on Sundays when they closed the road to vehicular traffic.

The throngs of people on all sorts of rolling devices amazed me. A hodgepodge of San Franciscans came out in shorts and stretch pants, cruising on bicycles and tricycles, various sorts of parents pushing strollers, young folks whizzing by on skateboards or unicycles, and multitudes of people on skates. We stopped at the blacktop of a basketball court where jumbo speakers blasted The Village People and the Bee Gees. Skaters flitted around, a bunch in a rolling conga line, and many individuals showing off their own personal disco moves as they spun and twisted to the beat.

I strapped on my skates, and then donned my kneepads, elbow pads, helmet, and gloves. You became my trainer as my body gave up the urge to step and replaced it with the necessary sway. I had my spills—never did figure out why they didn't make butt pads—and after a few weeks, I was skating along with the rest of them.

At first, you held my hand to give me support. Like a child, I'd venture off on my own, try a new turn, catch a little air, and glide back to you. We went every Sunday until I became as good a skater as you, and we still held hands those days because we wanted to. I'd never have done so in Guanajuato. The skates and your hand made me feel like a free bird again, like racing down the desert highway under a starry sky at a hundred miles an hour. In San Francisco, I felt a sense of liberty that I'd never approached in Phoenix or Guanajuato.

After skating, we'd walk through the AIDS Memorial Grove or get ice cream at Stow Lake. Once in a while, we'd walk Haight Street, and you'd buy overpriced used clothes, or we'd taste the giant tortilla-like bread and ground meat with sour cream at the African restaurant, or cop a chili dog at the diner. On those Sundays at the park and down in Haight-Ashbury, I forgot about Guanajuato and that I missed my family and my home. Or rather, I realized that I had a new family and a new home that did not replace the old ones but, at that moment, precluded them.

I thought of a bird and its nest—such a cliché. I imagined a little bird brought up in a circle of twigs. The parents work to keep it safe and feed it and teach it to fly. And one day, in response to instinct, it leaves. It has to leave. It has to build its own nest. I guess it hurts the little bird's heart for a while, yet to imagine it staying there in the home nest with mama and papa just isn't right. So there I was in San Francisco, and I had built my nest with you, or moved into one you had already gotten a good start on, anyway. But birds, like butterflies, know the way home.

I used to talk to Mamá once a week or so. You never minded the expense. At times, my talks with Mamá went on for an hour, though it usually seemed like ten minutes, and I could hardly remember what we'd talked about. She said once that talking to me was like talking to her best friend. She said she missed me, and that she felt pain sometimes. At first, I thought she meant the emotional kind.

She whispered it the first time. "No, I mean pain down there… when I go pee-pee… or try to."

"Mamá, that can't be good," I said.

She shushed me, as if concerned my empty house would find out, or all of Guanajuato would hear through the receiver.

"I haven't said anything to your papá."

"How long have you been experiencing that?" Mamá had always hated to bother anyone. The caretaker never needed any care herself.

"I don't know. Since a little while after you left."

"I've been gone for over a year!"

"Shh…."

"No shh…. You've got to see a doctor."

"It's just your papá has been stressed with the bills and all…."

"We'll… I'll make another deposit. It doesn't matter."

So began her kidney problems. And so began weekly trips to Western Union, giving money to drown my guilt, meager compensation for my absence.

She couldn't urinate, she couldn't sleep, and she started to suffer excruciating pain below her ribcage. After the first call, it took the better part of a month for the stone to pass, the doctor saying that at her age everything happened more slowly. She enjoyed a respite before another stone formed, and then another, and the doctor began to think there might have been more to it. Could be lead in her dishes, he'd said, or too much salt, or the aspirin she'd taken for everything, or the alcohol. Some kidney problems just seemed to happen in some people for genetic reasons.

By that time, I was in the other restaurant, and you and I had become somewhat estranged. I didn't say much at first, already aware of the stress you tended to take on. And I followed in Mamá's footsteps more than I ever cared to admit, not wanting to share the pain. I kept it inside and let it out those nights with Chuy and Chepa. To make matters worse, my visa had already expired. I knew going home was not an option, unless I was willing to run the risk of getting stuck down there. I was either stuck in the US or stuck in Mexico. Mamá had insisted that I not worry. She thanked me for the money and told me to stay put. After all, she'd said, "What would you do down here but be here and try to figure out how to make any money? I have people around me to help morally and to take me to the hospital. Of course I'd like to see you, but how else would we pay the doctor bills?"

Anyway, both Mamá and I hoped the problem would go away. The kidney stones passed, but her restlessness was replaced by weariness, and the doctor suggested more and more tests. I began to expect listlessness when I called Mamá, and I finally started hinting to you that Mamá's health seemed to be in decline. I knew you'd dig deeper, and at that point the whole story came out. I was sorry I disappointed you by not having shared it with you. I had my reasons.

You did everything you could possibly do. You insisted on contributing money. You researched kidney stones and chronic kidney disease online. You called the phone nurse and a doctor friend of yours. We had long talks about my family's health history. You did everything short of saying, "Here's a plane ticket. Go home." You knew and I knew that was not an option if we wanted to be together. Despite our setbacks, neither of us was ready to call it quits. Mamá had a point too—the most powerful form of love we could give had dollar signs in front of it. We stayed our course as long as we could until the list of options, like Mamá's health, began to truncate.

TWENTY-ONE

"I'VE already lost five pounds." Alberto's proud smile kept Joe from saying what he thought—only about two hundred pounds to go. It seemed Alberto's wardrobe had instantly changed to one of matching sweat suits. Joe wondered where they sold them in Alberto's size.

"You might just get a man yet," Joe said.

Alberto smiled sardonically before his face lit up as he changed the subject, "You know, I've been walking over at Golden Gate Park every day. Why don't you come with?"

Joe instantly shook his head at the mention of the park. "No, got to run the restaurant."

"Restaurant, restaurant. I've been telling you for months you need to get out. You look pale, Joe. Ghostly."

"Please, darling." Joe was about to let out one of the comments he had withheld.

"I'm just saying… it would do you some good. I mean, look at me… even Fat Albert is getting out." He gave a hearty Bill Cosby "Hey, hey, hey."

"It's good for you. I'm happy for you."

"It'll be good for you too. Quit resisting, let someone take over on a Wednesday evening—everyone here knows what they're doing—and say yes."

Joe sighed as he stood in thought. "Alright. I'll go. One time. I'm not promising to go with you every day. Weird things are still going on." The threatening phone calls hadn't entirely ceased.

"Okay. Seven o'clock at Stow Lake. Don't be late."

All day, Joe thought of the times at the park with Arturo. In their nearly five years together, some of his favorite memories were of the park. He had avoided going there, concerned that returning to the park would bring more emotions out of long-term storage than he could handle. Yet it hadn't taken much coaxing from Alberto for Joe to finally agree.

He took a taxi out to the lake and spotted Alberto in a bright orange getup that made him look like... an orange. Joe wore shorts, his white legs perhaps an equal target for friendly digs. Despite his concerns, he felt happy to be there and to simply hang out with someone. After all these years, he and Alberto had never seen each other outside the restaurant.

The October wind had picked up a tad. A few people in pedal boats drifted around on the lake. Ducks floated by and a few turtles sat on rocks and logs along the shore, soaking up the last bits of sunshine the day afforded.

"How old are you now?" Alberto asked out of the blue.

"Umm, twenty-seven."

Alberto looked at him askance.

Joe chuckled. "I mean thirty-seven."

The big man put his hands in the pockets of his sweatshirt. "Me... I'm going on fifty. And I just thought I'd have it all figured out by now."

"Yeah. Don't you hate when life gets in the way of your plans?"

"I'll say. Life... or maybe life's addictions."

"Okay, is this counseling hour again? You're not going to charge me, are you?"

"Come on, Joe. I'm not talking about you right now. Lately, the world's been revolving around me." He pulled his hand from his jacket and held up an index finger. "No... no astronomy jokes."

Joe bit his lip.

"But some people say that we're all victims of our own addictions, whatever they may be. Some people do drugs or alcohol, others become hoarders, some are workaholics—present company considered—and some of us overeat."

"So my addiction is overworking?"

"Well, we can have more than one addiction, you know. But don't you agree that working all the time sort of takes the place of something for you?"

"Someone, I guess."

"Yeah. Then again, you didn't think he'd live forever, did you? I mean, we all know that every relationship must end. And when that happens, what will take its place?"

"What about you? Are you ending your food addiction?"

Alberto veered his glance into the sky. He had always hated talking about food. "I'm trying," he finally said. "I know this stuff—it's all in the textbooks—but it's different when it's really you."

"And, what are you going to replace it with?"

"Crack cocaine?" He laughed. "No, hopefully not one addiction for another. If food has covered up any of my needs, it's probably just self-esteem. I hope I can replace it with just knowing I'm okay."

"Knowing you're okay?"

"Yeah. Peace."

The two continued around the lake in silence. Joe began to lose himself in the surroundings—the trees, the birds, children running and adults jogging. He'd hardly thought about Arturo even once. To their left, a lesbian couple walked by, holding hands. They brought to Joe's mind skating in the park with Arturo, though in place of the usual nostalgia he felt when he thought of Arturo, he tasted bitterness.

Even with Arturo, he'd had mixed feelings about holding hands, though he never mentioned it to him. Clif had liked holding hands, and he liked doing it in public, as he did kissing and flirting and anything else that might have offended the right-wingers who, to his way of thinking, had oppressed him all his life. It turned out that Clif was one of the main participants in the local chapter of ACT UP, the AIDS Coalition to Unleash Power. Clif's emphasis seemed to be on *unleash*.

At times, Chava's direct way of confronting everyone reminded Joe of Clif.

Joe had considered back then that Clif could present certain problems for him, a young man who depended on his Protestant family to whom he not yet come out. For a few months, he had succeeded in keeping the two extremes of his life completely separate. He'd seen Clif mostly at private functions Clif and his friends organized—barbecues, weekend hikes, and afternoon tea dances. Joe began to spend more time away from home and even skipped Bible study a few times on questionable pretexts. Joe had known that sooner or later the two trains would collide, but a part of him had bought a ticket and boarded for that very reason.

On his mother's birthday, the entire family had gone out to dinner—Mom and Dad, his four brothers and sisters, respective and respectful boyfriends and girlfriends. They were all young adults, Joe the perpetually single one. A couple waiters at the steakhouse came to the table at once. The prime rib and strip steaks had been grilled to bloody perfection. Of course, the family wasn't ready to eat the bounty until after the blessing. As the waiters continued to pass plates and condiments, Joe's dad cleared his throat and stretched his hands out to those beside him. Let the ritual begin, Joe thought, having for years found the public practice—a virtual séance—a dubious and somewhat embarrassing one. His diminishing belief in God was only confounded by the ritual that, in this case, made the waiters back off and stand still with hot, heavy plates in hand.

Joe, quiet and tolerant as always, grabbed the hand of his brother on one side and mother on the other. He thought of Clif, who, had he been there, would have been either laughing hysterically or exchanging heated arguments with Joe's dad. Joe had long known that his feigned faith was mostly backed by his loathing of confrontation and his economic necessity. Yet his family could choose their beliefs, and Joe had no right to oppose them. He laughed inside, and boiled at the thought that they would surely not show him the same tolerance and respect. He knew they'd never endure his holding hands in the place of his choice or with the person of his liking. Hypocrites, he thought of them. Hypocrite himself.

"Amen," his dad said.

"Amen," they repeated in unison. Joe's mouth barely moved. Hands went back down to laps and the waiting plates were finally presented.

"Bon appétit!" someone said.

They all dug in, steak knives cutting broiled flesh.

"How's school, Joseph? Didn't you just start?"

Joe hadn't picked up his silverware. His heart began to thump. He looked at his goblet of water, drops gathering around it.

"I think it's time to tell you," he said after clearing his throat like Daddy. The dinner party stopped, obviously not used to any assertions from him. "I'm…." A single cough cut his words. "I'm gay."

As if the waiter had just announced the steaks were not beef but horse meat, a wave of silent revulsion swept the party. Napkins covered mouths. Mother looked queasy.

"How could you," Daddy said, "on your mother's birthday?"

Could I retract it? Joe wondered. Should he? If not on Mother's birthday, then when? When would he be allowed to step up and be the way God made him? The devil's work, they would say. But God did not make abominations.

He could not take their revulsion. He left them, the dinner, and the white tablecloth and napkins. He walked home across Boise, embarrassed at his uncouth behavior, angry at himself, but even angrier at them for ever having made him so upset. He'd predicted their reaction correctly, which made him simultaneously laugh and despair.

He immediately packed and went to Clif's house. However, staying with Clif, Joe soon realized that they did not share the same ideas about monogamy. Joe couldn't help but feel like an imposition. Eventually, he understood that as Clif had used him for sex and fun, so Joe had used Clif to come out. They had too little in common. Before long, Joe found his own apartment, paid for by the Pell Grant and student loans, and shortly after graduating, had procured a job far from home and his family, in San Diego County. The job was uninteresting, but it was a foot in the door to the software industry and a lunging step away from the threshold of his youth.

"What, Joe? What are you thinking about?"

"Sorry, Alberto. Just got lost in times past."

"Peace," responded Alberto. "We'll find peace yet."

TWENTY-TWO

THE first *ofrenda* I can remember was an homage to Frida Kahlo. Grandma and my grandpa hadn't died yet, so Mamá had made it rather playful. She adorned it with as many copies of Frida Kahlo art as she could find, and she sat stuffed animal monkeys beside them to which she added thick eyebrows and moustaches with a black marker. I think she had chosen Frida because someone had given her a little Frida skeleton with the telltale brows and a moustache and a paintbrush. At the Monday swap meet, we found a bed from a dollhouse, and Mamá laid Frida in it. And then we wrote some of the poor woman's famous sayings—"I drank to drown my pain, but the damned pain learned how to swim," and "I hope the leaving is joyful; and I hope never to return." How the woman suffered after the terrible bus accident that left her broken and crippled. We'd written one quote that inspired me ever since I had heard it: "Feet, why do I need them if I have wings to fly?" I understood from her that we all have obstacles we can overcome if we choose to. The *ofrenda* was playful—we didn't know Frida personally, and we were just kids—but Mamá made sure we got something out of it.

During the weeks before the Day of the Dead, I would see the *calaveras* everywhere. In a way, they were meant to be funny, and they did make me laugh—skeletons dressed in everyday garb like that of the baker or the policeman or a school teacher or the undertaker, each with a huge smile of white pearly teeth. In some scenes, skeleton partygoers danced to the sounds of equally dead mariachis, in another scene, a skeletal cat crawled along the floor. Those *calaveras* and festivities took the fear out of death, in a way, by making it a regular part of life, all those people carrying on those things they did while alive. Of course, death isn't exactly like that. I don't cook anymore. Or drink.

Day of the Dead had its serious side too. After Grandma and my grandfather died, and Mamá was still sad for them, she changed the *ofrenda*. No more playful facial hair, no more laughing skeletons. Instead, she placed the olives and *conchas* there, and pictures of her parents, and she would kneel sometimes in front of the table with candles lit. She'd say silent prayers and cross herself and walk around, melancholy. We'd all go take a trip out to the cemetery on the second of November and leave flowers for them at their gravesite. The family would crouch in the weedy grass and look sad. By the third or fourth of November, the *ofrenda* would be taken down, and Mamá would be back to normal, as if she had expended enough tears for them that year, and our lives went back to normal.

In Phoenix, I had imagined Halloween would be pretty much the same as the Day of the Dead. Then I learned that what was once a pagan ritual to ward off evil spirits had been converted over time into a joint venture where candy companies and children conspired to get adults to buy candy and give it to them for dressing ridiculously. My first year in San Francisco, I figured we'd be waiting at the door to give out treats. Later I learned San Francisco had its own variation. Not for mourning or remembering our loved ones, not for candy or profiteering via tooth decay, but for letting out, as Alberto would have said, our alter egos!

Halloween seemed like the one time a year you'd let yourself go crazy, amor. Once I got the idea, I embraced it. I'm not sure what it meant that we both decided to dress in drag. Somehow I thought someone should be a man, but once we got into preparing, all expectations around gender roles, at least for that night, went out the window. Suddenly, Chava had become my mentor. He plucked my eyebrows, shaved my legs, and applied my makeup. Where he learned to set a wig, I never knew. He even gave me a crash course on walking in heels—a feat for neither the acrophobic nor the inebriated.

We started walking down to the Castro. My feet couldn't handle the hills in heels so I took them off, giggly and concerned about my nylons. We'd already had a few drinks. I heard some noise from the people gathering up ahead a few blocks, and when we reached the corner of Castro Street and 18th, I nearly fainted—Castro Street had become the Festival Cervantino in drag. People of all colors, clad in all colors, packed the street from one side to the other. I pushed my purse up on my shoulder, grabbed your hand in one of mine and Chava's in the other, and said, "Part the ocean, girls, this fish is ready to swim!"

Before long, we were dancing in the thick of drag queens as tall as posts and as hairy as beasts. Leather daddies walked around with chaps in the front and nothing behind. People of all ages strutted in every imaginable costume. A breastless cancer survivor displayed her chest. Youngsters climbed up trees and on top of the bus stops and danced to Madonna and Cyndi Lauper tunes blaring from speakers on platforms, as I sang along, "Girls chust wan to have fun, oh, girls chust wan to have fun!"

Your hand slipped away from mine. In an instant, you were lost from me in the sea. At the Cervantino, you were the tallest and whitest in the crowd, but here you were just another gabacho in a frock. Behind me, Chava's face oscillated between carefree cheer and defensive paranoia. I'd let him go a minute before so I could hold my beer and keep steady on the heels at the same time. I wondered where you were or where I'd find you. I guessed I'd spend the rest of the night alone with just Chava. Then your hand found me between bouncing bodies and pulled me toward you. Chava pushed close behind, and we were together again. You'd procured another round of beer somehow, and the party continued.

Half past really late, we stumbled up the stairs at home. I'd lost my heels and torn my pantyhose. My wig twisted backward. My lipstick was gone and the shadow of my beard probably looked darker than my eye shadow. *Thank God I'm a man*, I thought. We were laughing hard, tired from excitement. I threw my purse on the sofa beside Chava, who had just passed out on it. You took my hand and started leading me to the bedroom. On the way there, I stopped in front of the *ofrenda* to Grandma and my grandfather. I looked at the blue and white *calavera* I had placed there and took a bite of sweet bread before I snuffed out the candle. Their picture reminded me of who I usually was.

Two days later, and dressed so they'd recognize me, I knelt before the *ofrenda* like Mamá always had. I spoke to them, mostly Grandma, thanking her for the dedication she had showed me. And I sang a lullaby she'd always sing to me at bedtime.

Until tomorrow
If God desires
That I sleep well
The time for bed has come
And to dream also
Because tomorrow will be another day
And we must live it with joy.

"If God desires." I must have heard that fifty times a day growing up. "I'll see you tomorrow," someone would say. "If God desires," the other would answer. There was a meaning in the phrase that hadn't occurred to me until that moment, a message and a reminder. You never know when your time will come. Life is precarious. Enjoy it. Yours could be the picture on next year's *ofrenda* on the Day of the Dead.

TWENTY-THREE

SOMETHING smelled like shit. It reminded Joe of an unhappy customer's complaint earlier in the day. Of course, he hadn't taken her comment literally. There on the front porch of the house, something really smelled like excrement. He wondered if a dog had come up and crapped right on the landing, or if a neighbor or maybe Chava had stepped in it and tracked it up. He raised his foot behind him to check his soles and he could barely see in the dimness of the porch light. The smell came from in front of him, not from behind, so he was pretty sure it hadn't been him.

When he pushed the door open—glass intact, he noted—a powerful waft of fecal aroma overwhelmed him. There at the base of the stairs lay a mound of poop that had been crammed through the mailbox slot. He put his hand up to his mouth like a makeshift gasmask and flicked the light switch with the other. A nasty customer complaint, nearly sixty dollars missing from the till, and now this, a load of shit atop the mail on the floor. "Chava!" he screamed up the stairs. No answer. He took a lunge over the mess and charged upstairs.

Joe could tell instantly that Chava had already arrived home. He'd left the restaurant hours before, and now he'd left the hallway light on again. He must have known about the load downstairs. Fury rose to Joe's temple like steam in a pressure cooker. He went directly to Chava's bedroom door with half a mind to throw him out right then and there. He lifted his fist to bang on the door but detained himself when he heard Chava's voice, in Spanish, raised higher than his own. "Fine! I'll have the money to you as soon as I can!"

By the sound of it, Chava shared Joe's rage. He must have seen the atrocity and rushed upstairs to make the call. Joe took a deep breath and tried to temper himself before he did or said something he'd later regret. Near the door sat the *ofrenda* to Arturo. Joe tried to feel the soothing hands of his lover upon his shoulders to help him through the incident. Holding back the fury, he knocked on the door.

Chava opened immediately. "What?"

"Well, what did he say?"

"What did who say?"

"Dario. Who else? The one who left that shit down there, I'm sure."

"What shit?"

Joe's shoulders fell in disbelief. "Are you kidding me? Didn't you see what's down there?"

"No. I came up to handle a few things. I've been on the phone a while. I haven't been down there."

"Well, then, it happened while you were here!"

Chava came out of his room and peered down the stairs. "Gross. What is it? You can smell it from up here."

"What do you think? Obviously, Dario came by... or sent someone by and took his revenge on you again. You keep saying you're going to handle it. You keep making these phone calls. I'm going over to his house right now to talk to him."

"Joe, listen. This thing with Dario is not that big a deal. I'll go take care of it for once and for all." Chava went back into his room, dug through his things, and put on a flannel shirt he pulled from a mound of clothes.

"What am I supposed to do?" Joe said.

"Nothing. You're just supposed to let me take care of things, as I told you. It's not what you think."

"I wasn't asking you," Joe said, looking at the *ofrenda*. "I wish Arturo would tell me."

"He might tell you to make up your own mind for once," Chava said as he whisked by in a flash of plaid. "I'm sorry about this. Leave it if you want. I'll clean it later. I'm going over there right now to fix this." He tromped down the stairs and slammed the door behind him.

Fix it? It had been almost a month since Chava had moved in, and they were still getting phone calls and dealing with this… shit. He went into the washroom behind the kitchen for a broom and dustpan. Though Chava had promised to clean it up, Joe wasn't about to let it stink up the place any longer. It wouldn't be the first time he'd cleaned up someone's shit, and it likely wouldn't be the last.

As he tried to sort any important mail from the soiled stuff and the junk mail, he started thinking. He couldn't believe that he had let Chava in along with all of his problems. And then the kid kept playing off this thing with Dario and promising to take care of it. Joe had been worried Chava would go over there and murder the guy, but now he decided Chava was simply shining him on. For all Joe knew, Chava owed him thousands, or had even stolen from him. Great, a thief in his house! His temper started boiling again.

"You're right," Joe said aloud. "I'll make up my own mind. I'll talk to the motherfucker and get to the bottom of this myself." He dropped the broom where he stood and went back up the stairs to get the phone in Chava's bedroom. Cocky kid thought he was such a macho and that he could take on the world by himself. All he really did was bring trouble. Joe picked up the phone, hit the button for a dial tone, and immediately punched the redial button. "Never thought of that, did you?" Joe said smugly.

The phone rang a few times and finally picked up. "*Bueno?*" A woman's voice.

"I need to speak with Dario," Joe said in Spanish.

"Dario? You must have the wrong number." Joe looked at the screen on the phone and saw an area code unfamiliar to him. The lady hung up. The number disappeared. So did his train of thought. Who was the woman? What happened to Dario? Could Chava be mixed up in more than Joe had ever imagined?

Dumbfounded and unsure what to do, he returned to where he had left the broom and dustpan and decided to finish cleaning up the shit. Most of the letters he swept right into the dustpan—almost none of his official dealings were handled through actual paper correspondence anymore. Advertisements, some sort of gem fair, and something unusual. For a second he thought it was a picture of poop and then made out, in the dim light, a postcard of a picture of a potato. He checked it for unsanitary residue, flipped it over, and immediately recognized his mother's curly handwriting after all these years. He left the broom again and hiked up to the kitchen.

> *Dear Joseph,*
>
> *It's been forever. Your daddy and I are fine. He's going on ten years retired now and his pension finally came through. We changed the linoleum in the kitchen. Your sister came over with her three children. She gave me your address. I hope you don't mind I'm writing.*
>
> *She also told us about your partner. Your daddy and I are sorry. It must be hard to lose someone you love. I couldn't imagine losing your daddy.*
>
> *It's time we spoke again. We may have lots of differences but we have only one family. If we can't count on family to get us through the hard times, then who can we count on?*
>
> *Your daddy sends his best. God bless.*
>
> *Love, Mom*

She stamped the bottom with an angel, its wings spread wide across her signature. Joe could remember her stamp kit in a big white tackle box of arts and crafts supplies. He smiled, picturing his mother at her table. Who wrote postcards anymore? Knowing her, she probably didn't have an e-mail account, let alone Facebook, Twitter, or any such modern thing. For all he knew, they didn't even own a computer.

His sister Cindy was the middle one, and was always in the middle of everyone, trying to make peace. He'd known she'd gotten married, after half suspecting she was a dyke, and had heard about her first two children, not the third. He pictured their get-together and the blessing of the food over a great big table. His mother would tell the grandchildren to sit up straight while his father would scold them for running in the house, sporting untucked shirts, or disobeying some other important rule. It had been a long, long time.

After he had left for San Diego, it seemed the distance reflected the state of their relationship. That distance facilitated the familial breakup, in a way—it provided the perfect rationale for their contact to dwindle. At first, he'd call every month or so, and catch up with his mother. He'd call his daddy and siblings on birthdays. Even those calls became fewer with more years in between, until eventually they ceased almost entirely. Cindy was the exception. Somehow, as a librarian, she seemed to have swung slightly over to the left from Mother and Daddy. If she could only leash in those wild terrors of children, she might have been more likeable, visitable. Once Arturo came into Joe's life, and the restaurant came into existence, Joe's inclination to maintain any relationship with his family had disappeared.

He read the card over and over again. *Partner*. Joe could scarcely believe she had gotten her hand to write the word. And *someone you love*. It blew him away. They still had differences, though, to which she clearly alluded. True, a person had only one family, but Joe considered his new family in San Francisco a decent surrogate. He still felt some bitterness about everything that had happened. She had made an effort, reached out her hand through the postal system, and even dodged a lump of shit to get here. But it was three years too late. He was handling the problem with his new family. What assistance could she or any of his family possibly give him?

He walked the postcard over to Arturo's *ofrenda*. He smiled. There was a certain delight in seeing those words—*partner, someone you love*. "Arturo," he said, "I think this postcard is for you." He propped it against the candle and went to bed.

TWENTY-FOUR

MAMÁ used to cry all the time. People made fun of her for it. She cried at church for particularly inspiring sermons, she cried at birthdays and graduations and weddings, she cried at holidays when people she hadn't seen for ages would come to visit, she cried watching romantic movies, or sad ones, or happy ones, and if anyone gave her a gift of any sort, forget about it. I was sure Mamá used more facial tissue than toilet paper.

But the first time I heard Mamá *really* cry, it cut through my coat and shirt and the skin on my chest. It opened my ribs like the lid of a piano and plucked the most painful chord inside. That cry, different from her usual overemotional outbursts, was more of a wail, but a softened one, dulled by her pressed lips, the closed door, the energy robbed from her by the ailment that distressed her. Tears came to my eyes as soon as I realized what the origin was of the muffled sound. I did not knock on the door, or hope to console her, because I was aware of my own impotence, my inability to do anything to help her, the same feeling that must have overtaken her. My papá went inside, doubtless as unable to take away her pain as me, and I saw her lying on the floor, her knees bent in such a way that I imagined she had been kneeling, praying, until her body gave out and fell sideways to the cold tile.

My sister Miriam had suffered an extreme headache. They gave her aspirin at first, and asked her about her menstrual cycle, or any exam coming up at school for which she hadn't studied. After a day in bed, a fever took her. Her body alternated between sweating and becoming rigid and shaky with chills, and she became delirious. It took a full day before they called a doctor, who insisted they bring her to the hospital. My papá worried about the money, for we had little, but Mamá said we'd pawn everything as long as God would keep my sister alive. Our family had already been through the burials of my grandparents, and the expense of that, and my papá always feared someone would come and take the house. Trust in God, she said, He will provide somehow. So they took my sister away in a neighbor's car and left her in the small emergency room of the local hospital.

I imagined Miriam's *ofrenda*. Would we use the doll-sized hospital bed Mamá had used for the Frida Kahlo *ofrenda*? Would there be another *calavera*? Would we keep a cracked coconut stuffed with strips of pig skin topped with chile sauce and lemon juice beside Grandma's olives? I felt bad for wondering about those things.

In reality, I hadn't been particularly close to my sister. I was two and a half years older than she—an eternity for children—and she a girl, I a boy. Sometimes I had resented her—having to watch out for her and stick up for her, having to stay at home at times for her and babysit. Later I even felt envious of her, jealous that she was a girl and could have boyfriends and I couldn't. I felt a secret satisfaction when my papá restricted her and told boys to go home and to not come to the house any more. And then sometimes Mamá would teach her how to cook, but I listened and learned better than she did. Now I noticed that her impending death had a way of erasing some of the petty rivalries, as would time later on.

Mamá and my papá came home from the hospital together. Papá reminded her that the doctor insisted Mamá get some rest because Miriam would need her mother to be strong. Some neighbors came by. A family friend brought up meningitis—a cousin of hers around Miriam's age had recently been afflicted and died of it. Mamá's tears began, the boisterous cry she used in public, not the gut-wrenching, muffled wail. I mostly stayed in my room. It wasn't until they had left and my papá had gone to sleep that I heard her guttural moans. It made me feel so sick to my stomach, I feared for a moment I had contracted the fever from my sister. And I realized we were all mortal—we would all die one day and that the unease in my stomach had descended from the ache tugging in my heart, and from the precocious awareness of my own weakness and eventual death. It made me think then of my own *ofrenda* and what they would put on it. Would Mamá yowl for me? Would my papá worry about the money?

My sister didn't die. She stayed in the hospital for three or four nights. I stayed home from school and went with Mamá to the hospital instead. My papá stuck to his way of fathering—he worked extra to pay the medical bills. He kept food on the table while everyone else worried.

Cousins and aunts from afar called to ask about Miriam. Friends and neighbors visited and inquired. Instead of sitting and waiting to be served, as usual, they sat Mamá on the couch, and brought food and drink themselves. A young teenager, I was there, regarded with smiles and hugs. Sometimes it seemed they didn't know what to say to me. Someone asked me if I was worried, if I missed her. I shrugged. Teenagers are so focused on their own burgeoning lives. But I noticed the way they came together—family and friends, young and old, women and men—not unlike a funeral. And I saw how the sadness and fear became a unifying force sealed with hugs and smiles and nourishment. The bad time brought people together.

Years later, when I was in San Francisco, it was Mamá who had become sick. The occasional bouts of pain continued, as did the general fatigue. After a few months, the doctors diagnosed her with chronic kidney disease. You and I sent money. Thank God the restaurant was doing well enough. And it was me this time who felt quiet and distraught, helpless to do anything but visit the Western Union office during business hours, and I knelt on the floor in prayer and sometimes wanted to fall to one side. And it was Miriam who would come to Mamá's rescue. I was happy then that she had moved in with her boyfriend and settled in Guanajuato, roots taking hold at home while my roots reached out. And I still felt some resentment too, for Miriam's being able to be with Mamá while I was so far from home.

Everything in the universe tends toward round, like a rock in a river that stumbles along, carried by the current. The most jagged and misshapen pieces eventually evolve into spheres. Then all those circles get swallowed by the round earth and resurface sometime later and start all over again. We can't always see the circles when we're standing on their very surface. Now I see it. Now I see everything.

TWENTY-FIVE

CHAVA hadn't returned the night he left. Joe could only imagine the shit, had he not picked it up, still down on the landing… and the smell of it. Perhaps Alberto was right—Joe needed to set the limits and maintain them. And now Chava had left to go "take care of things." For all Joe knew, Chava would go right back to Dario, disregard Joe, and continue whatever it was they had.

Joe spent his morning dallying around the restaurant. He noticed with some reassurance that the few times he'd left the place to the employees, the roof hadn't fallen in, the register hadn't been robbed, and the health inspectors hadn't shut the place down. Perhaps he'd been a bit addicted to work, or had let his insecurities manifest themselves there. He hated when Alberto was right, which was most of the time. The big man had told him to trust in his employees, to take a break, and to set limits—strict boundaries—with Chava. Joe had always been able to throw it back at Alberto, at least internally, knowing that the big man didn't take his own advice. But Alberto had been sticking to his diet to the point where Joe could actually see a change in his weight, so what could he throw back now?

Joe looked up to see heavy strings of cobwebs around the butterflies on the wall and a huge, dangling spider coming down to attack whoever passed by. One of the employees had taken it upon herself to decorate for Halloween. She must have found the old box of decorations back in the storeroom. Only three more days until Halloween… and two more after that until the Day of the Dead. He hadn't made any plans whatsoever. By default, he'd work at the restaurant, maybe get a few huge bags of candies to pass out to children from the restaurant door. The Day of the Dead would be the same default, except he'd find some time to sit by the *ofrenda* at home, put some fresh flowers on it, and talk with Arturo for a while. On the Day of the Dead, for the last two years, Joe had always felt a certain closeness with Arturo, wherever he was, that he couldn't achieve on any other day, as if it were the anniversary of his death, a memorial day.

The phone at the podium rang. He'd still been receiving crank calls and was half tempted to not answer. Business was business, though, and whoever made those calls must know he'd have no choice but to keep answering. Chava might have been right, too, about Dario being a pussy. After over a year with Chava and all this time of crank phone calls, graffiti, and cramming shit through the mailbox, Joe didn't even know what the guy looked like. His tactics demonstrated cowardice. And persistence. In one sense, Joe felt like he deserved to know the details of their relationship despite the way Chava coveted his privacy. In another sense, Joe didn't want to hear it. He could imagine. Sure, he'd made assumptions, including the assumption that meeting the guy would only confirm all the things that made the relationship between Chava and Dario a sick one.

"José Arturo Amor," he answered, half waiting for the click and the droning vacancy of the dial tone. "Can I help you?"

"It's me, Joe. It's Chava."

"You need to hurry up," Joe said, looking up at the clock. "You're gonna be late."

"Listen. I need to talk to you."

"Chava. Are you serious? Where are you?"

"At home."

"Home? You mean my home or what?"

"Yes. Where else?"

"And what, you're not coming in? Some emergency, right? Another crisis."

"This is different. Um, can you just listen?"

"Okay, what?"

"I mean here. Can you come home? If you've ever been like a father to me, be it now."

Goose bumps rose on Joe's arms and crown. A part of him suspected he was getting played... again. Another part of him, a weaker part, he thought, couldn't deny a request like that. Strict boundaries? Joe's father had drawn strict boundaries and what good did that do? In these situations, he preferred to err on the side of tolerance—permissiveness, in some people's eyes. Joe wouldn't be the one to send Chava away out of stubbornness. "Okay. Let me get someone in charge here and I'll be there in a few minutes. Don't leave!"

As he walked up the street, Joe alternated between anger, concern, and curiosity. Arturo had always given the kid a break, talking about his upbringing, his absent dad, his desperate mother, his challenging siblings, and their poverty. It was all true. But when should a person be expected to move on from a past like that? Never? No, Chava would have to take responsibility for himself. At twenty-two, he was no child anymore.

Step by step, Arturo would say. Joe could almost hear Arturo's pleading voice come to him in whispers on the wind. "He's made progress, José. Show him love he hasn't had." Those were the words from the only one of the three who had really been shown parental love as a child. Arturo had always achieved both patience and decisiveness, somehow, while Joe tore himself apart between wavering points of view and their respective courses of action.

When he reached the door of the house, he noticed some dried scrapings of feces on the ledge of the mail slot. Chava's voice rang in his ears: "This is different." Seemed like the same charade to Joe. Now what? He feared Chava was going to confess a crime, admit a drug problem, or ask Joe for money.

He climbed the stairs apprehensively, glanced at the *ofrenda* for a moment before peering through Chava's door to find him sitting on the bed with his face in his hands. Joe felt torn again—he had the urge to immediately approach and comfort him, and yet he held back, wanting to stand firm, while awaiting the onslaught of bad news and the subsequent, impudent request for Joe to save him somehow.

"Yes, Chava?" Joe's tempered voice reflected the middle ground.

"I don't know what to do."

Joe sighed and leaned against the frame of the door, hoping he was mistaken, but bracing for the worst. "What happened? Just tell me how much you owe him... or tell me you guys are in trouble. What kind of trouble? Say it like it is. There must be a solution."

Chava looked up to him from the bed with irritation, angry tiger eyes, the anger turning then to confusion. "What the fuck are you talking about?"

Joe rolled his eyes. "Dario. What the hell has happened with Dario?" Joe started to let his frustration out. "You've been playing it off, telling me you're going to fix it. But all I hear is the phone calls behind your closed door. Money! And I get crank-called and get shit stuffed through my front door!"

"Are you talking about Dario? I told you he's a pussy. I told you I would handle it and I did. You have no trust in me!"

"Have you earned it? You can't even show up to work on time! Then you say you'll take care of it and the restaurant gets spray-painted!"

"Now you're being an idiot. The cops told you it could be anybody. Get off it, Joe. It's handled. Dario won't bug you no more."

"How do I know that? You've said it before. Did you pay him finally?"

"It ain't about money," Chava snapped. "Okay. It's over with him!"

"How can you know? How can you be so sure?"

"Because I made *him* my fucking bitch!"

"What?" Joe's voice ratcheted down a few notches.

"I told you he's a pussy. Always thought he was so tough, always wanting a piece of my ass. I finally gave the little-dicked mothafucka what he needed—I went there last night, turned him around, and fucked his shit until he couldn't take it no mo'. Yelping and screaming, 'Please stop!' The pussy-boy cried and howled. I didn't care... I punished him, smacked him, and spanked him. He couldn't take it. It's over."

Joe wiped his face with his hand as if attempting to erase his confusion. "That's not what I thought you were going to say." He let out a smile and a bit of relief.

"That's what you get for assuming you know it all."

"Okay. So that's it?"

"No. It's not even the problem. Sometimes you're so blind, Joe."

"Maybe blind, but not deaf. I hear your phone calls, but you don't tell me anything, so how should I know?"

"You don't want to know." Chava put his face in his hands again. "I don't even want to know."

Joe sat on the bed beside Chava and put his arm around his shoulder. "Tell me, and let's figure it out together."

Chava stood up. Joe's hand fell to the bedspread. "It's my fucking family, my amá."

"Oh, I didn't realize you were talking to her."

"Where do you think all my money went?"

The recurring vision of Chava with his lines of coke, bottles of booze, and downtown disco clubs appeared in Joe's head. "I wasn't sure," he said.

Chava looked up at him like a lost child.

"So, what happened with your mother?"

"Well, we always talked, you know. Even after I came here to San Francisco, I still called her sometimes. And I would send her money because she had, like, bills to pay, and my brothers and sister always had some problem."

"Oh."

"You know. I felt kind of bad being so far away. I mean, I can't be there, but it sucks when she gets stressed out and stuff about money. So I would send what I had. But then she probably gives some to my papá for liquor and shit.

"So, a couple weeks ago, she told me my fucking brother is up for parole and would I go over there and vouch for him. Like, she wants me to tell the judge or whoever that he's a good guy. I said I'm not going. And she says we need to help him turn around."

"Are you going? Do you need time off?" Joe asked.

"I told her hell no. I ain't going. She says why, because I ought to help my brother. He's getting better and shit." The tears in Chava's eyes belied the anger in his brow. His voice quavered, and he started to talk as if into space. "*Turn around*? Where was he when his friends told me to turn around? He knew what they were doing. Probably thought it was funny. Fuck, he probably offered me out to them—a little fairy ass for the takin', right? How many times? How many of them?" Chava yelled and cried simultaneously. "Fucking macho cholos! They all wanted an easy piece. And I had better shut up about it too!"

"I don't know what to say," Joe said meekly from the bed. "I'm sorry."

"I know. There's nothing to say. Why do you think I never said anything?" He folded his arms and bowed his head, his voice still quivering. "I just keep it inside and try to forget about it. But now I can't believe she's expecting me to go help him."

"You don't have to."

Silence. Joe looked at the wall and then back at Chava, who continued staring into space, his boyish face lit by the light from the window.

"It was like he had to be cool." The sudden calmness of Chava's voice thinned the heavy air, and Joe saw the way Chava tried so hard to forget about it. "He couldn't let down his cholo friends, like a stupid gang. And their pact of silence. He couldn't let down the 'homies'. One time he says to me, after they did it, like, four or five times, he says, 'Are you okay, bro?' What was I supposed to say? I just sort of moved my head. Of course I wasn't okay! I was eleven or twelve!"

"Maybe he did care," Joe said after a pause. "I mean, why did he say that? Maybe he just felt like he couldn't do anything. He couldn't go against them."

"He should have," Chava said sternly, but with a look of sadness in his eyes. "He should have protected me. Now he wants me to help him."

"Yeah, he should have protected you."

"I don't know. Maybe he would have if he could. There was one time he gave me a few bucks to go to the mall before they got there. 'Get out of here,' he said."

"Maybe that's all he could do. I mean, he was only what, sixteen or so, right?"

"Yeah, something like that."

"Kids don't always know. Hell, adults don't always know. And it's been a long time now."

"I know. And my amá keeps begging me. She says I'm the decent one, that the judge will look better at me, and she hates going to court and stuff."

"You haven't seen her for the longest."

"Not since I got to San Francisco."

Joe thought of his mother, and the two decades in which he hadn't seen her. He wouldn't wish that on anyone.

"What do you think I should do? Do you think I should go and help him?"

Another tough decision. Joe hated them. Arturo would have answered by now while Joe remained thinking about it. Joe considered the *ofrenda*, and the way Arturo always knew. And then he thought of the postcard from his mother. *We have only one family.*

"Yes, I think you should go," he answered firmly, "if for nothing more than to see your mother. For all you know, they won't give him parole anyway."

"Okay. You're probably right." He lifted his head and humbly asked, "So can I have a few days off?"

"Of course, Chava. It's the least I can do."

The young man immediately pulled a bag from the closet and began to get some clothes together, as if he'd been waiting for permission, or waiting for a decision.

Arturo's smirking face came to Joe's head. Okay, Joe admitted, so he didn't make the decision by himself again. His mother had something to do with it. He wondered if decisions were ever truly independent? *Even when we rebel, as Chava had in so many ways, we do so in a manner opposing those who have opposed us. Nobody is independent,* Joe thought. *We're all connected.*

TWENTY-SIX

A DONATION? It made me think of the tithing basket at the church, or spare change tossed at a homeless guy on the street. It couldn't be that my sister was planning an organ donation, and certainly not one to be done by a doctor down in Mexico.

The kidney disease had progressed rapidly. In a few short years, the diagnosis had changed from an infection in the urinary tract, to kidney stones, to chronic kidney disease, and now kidney failure. Both kidneys had been severely damaged. The words cut like a guillotine—failure. Mamá had always been the strong one, infallible. As the months passed, we hoped for a cure, or at least a respite. Nothing. It only worsened. I heard my sister's voice saying the doctors had concluded she was a match.

After years of listening to your criticism about the doctors in Mexico, I had become skeptical. Sure, they could set a broken bone or deliver a baby. They'd handled Miriam's flu successfully enough. But an organ transplant seemed like a completely different ballgame.

I remember how you watched me. My face surely had gone pale as I talked on the phone. It made the color in your face vanish too. The money we had sent, all my prayers, had been futile. And now a transplant. There wasn't much time, they had said, and not much hope. Mamá's body could reject it. Either Mamá or Miriam could die, or both.

The phone call came late at night. We had been playing Yahtzee in the living room. We'd had a couple of drinks. You had just rolled five ones and you were celebrating. When the phone rang, I hadn't guessed it was my family. It was late, and besides, we always made the calls to reduce their phone bill. They never called. After I hung up, you swallowed hard and looked nauseous, as if those words had kicked you in the stomach. You didn't even write down your fifty points, and I know how you loved to have your Yahtzee boxes all pretty and perfectly filled in. You knew this time the situation had gone over an invisible line. I'd have to leave.

An hour later, a little after midnight, you came into the bedroom with an airline ticket you'd printed on the all-in-one in the study. I had already started packing. You watched me in silence, and pulled underwear from the drawer for me. I didn't console you or calm your worries because I worried about the same thing—I might not be able to come back. I found my Mexican passport and my American tourist visa, both expired, and put them in my carry-on. You gave me one of your credit cards and some cash.

I had till the next afternoon before the flight for San Miguel de Allende would take off. I thought about making love to you, like an act of farewell, but I was preoccupied with my mother, the trip, and getting back. It didn't happen. The last time we had done it, I couldn't have imagined that it would be the last time I would touch your skin like that, and the parts of you that were territory exclusive to me, my symbolic terrain. We had to try to get some rest. We were both emotionally drained. So we lay in the bed and held each other, our eyes closing, our frightening thoughts at times reopening them.

You went to work early but pulled away from the restaurant in time to accompany me in the taxi to the airport. You came to the counter with me and all the way up to the security checkpoint. We hugged for minutes, oblivious to everything around us. The reverse had been so easy for so long—minding everything around us and being oblivious to each other—when there was no immediate threat. "Good luck. Let's hope you get your visa. And my best wishes to your family." You smiled at me wanly, and touched my ear. I was sure my family had already felt your best wishes—they must have known all the money we sent wasn't just from me. I was less sure about the visa. You swallowed and said, "Good-bye."

I touched your ear back. "Not good-bye. I'm not saying good-bye. Until later. I will see you again." I hoisted the carry-on up on my shoulder like the purse at Halloween. This time, the fish wasn't about to swim. Rather, the bird was about to fly, about to migrate home.

As I waited for the boarding time, I had the urge to go back to you already. I knew there would be little I could do in Guanajuato but be anxious, try to console my inconsolable father, and wait at the hospital. I could have walked out of the airport the same way I came, no border patrol to hassle me, no immigration checks, and no closed gates. I empathized for you and those times you had struggled with hard choices. Because the other option was that Mamá or Miriam would die, or both of them, while I sat safely in the northern nest, waiting for a simple phone call, a report, as I sipped a margarita. If I had learned anything from Catholicism, it was that one sacrificed. I fought the urge to run to you, catch your yellow taxi, as I handed the attendant my boarding pass. I squeezed it hard for a split second before I let go of it, and listened to the beep as she scanned the barcode. And then I was off, on a one-way ticket to Guanajuato, and to Mamá.

I walked into an empty living room that evening. The door was closed but had been left unlocked. I set my things down in my old room. Dust rose up from the blanket. Soon I would find out that Mamá had been in the hospital for over a month. I would feel once again like a child, left alone because people felt awkward, not knowing what to say, or not wanting to say it. I expected someone would walk by and pat my head.

The streets in Guanajuato seemed deserted. I knocked on a neighbor's door. She hugged me, said how sorry she was, and told me which hospital to go to. I hadn't called to let them know I was coming because someone might have talked me out of it. I left the house and made my way to the hospital.

My papá was there alone. Our family seemed so small now, reduced. Where were all the cousins and aunts and uncles? All too far, or too busy, or old, or poor. He gave me a metallic hug, firm but cold. I wondered if he felt less than manly accepting the money we'd been sending. He would have never kept up with those kinds of bills. I hadn't seen him for five years, yet he looked fifteen years older. His hair had grayed, his eyes were sunken, and his skin was wrinkled.

"They're prepped for tomorrow," he said. "Both sleeping now."

"Tomorrow?" I had come just in time.

"First thing in the morning. A specialist is coming in from the city, and some students also, to watch. The organ match was right, now all that's left is God's opinion."

I saw a sadness in my papá's eyes I did not recognize. Somehow we always must have assumed he would be the first to go. If she left him, how could he not wither away like an untended plant?

A nurse let me peek into Mamá's room from the darkness of the corridor. They had suppressed her immune system in preparation for the organ so her body wouldn't attack it like the Aztecs did the *conquistadores*. Her eyes were shut, a machine beeped. The nurse said it was better for everybody that we go home and get rested.

My papá and I ate a late dinner of room-temperature *huaraches*. They'd been brought by a neighbor and left out on the counter, covered with foil. The refried beans had dried and cracked like the floor of a desert, the edges of the cilantro leaves had blackened, and the diced onions emitted pungent fumes that burned my nasal canal. The thick, oblong tortilla was as tough as the leather sandal it was named for, and about as flavorful. Neither my papá nor I had felt in the mood to go out to get something dazzling or delicious. And given the circumstances, satisfying a superficial craving would have seemed rude.

You called me late that night. We exchanged stories about our days, you at the restaurant and me traversing half of the western hemisphere. You told me you missed me. I remember your voice was so clear on the phone I felt like we were in the same room together, yet at the same time, I felt like I was in a completely different world. Like now.

TWENTY-SEVEN

SITTING in the back of a yellow taxi, Joe had stolen a couple of glances at Chava, whose eyes, behind long, dark eyelashes, were fixed in a childlike stare. His close-cropped hair was like the fuzz of a ripening peach, while the scar above his eye, the one on his chin, and those hacked dashes of eyebrows were like bruises on the fruit. They shared little conversation on the ride to the bus station, as if Chava's instincts had told him to shut up after his rare bout of self-disclosure. Joe felt dutiful, however, accompanying Chava in the taxi as he went off to deal with family matters, and to face his mother.

Outside the Greyhound station, a handful of people waited, a couple standing at the curb, a few leaning against the wall, smoking. Chava leaned over and gave Joe an unexpected hug followed by a kiss on the cheek. He got out of the car quietly and slung his bag over his shoulder. "Fucking faggot," one of the people on the curb said. Joe held his breath, waiting for Chava's explosion of wallops to occur, but he passed them as if he hadn't even noticed. The taxi left the scene, and Joe turned in his seat and watched Chava enter the building and disappear from his life.

The yellow taxi was impressively clean, the paint shiny and the upholstery vacuumed, much as the taxi had been that had taken him and Arturo to the airport three years before. It made him think of a hearse, freshly washed, as it drove on to its passenger's final resting place. The taxi back in Guanajuato that had taken them to the airport in San Miguel de Allende for the flight to the US had been a decrepit old thing, but the emotions that day, just over seven years ago, had been of excitement and anticipation, a harsh contrast to these fateful trips to San Francisco air terminals and bus terminals.

He remembered the look on Arturo's face after the phone rang during their table game. "A transplant?" Arturo had repeated, with a twisted, confused brow. It seemed he could hardly believe his ears, as if doctors in Mexico were incapable of such a surgery, or his mother incapable of such a need. For Joe, it had been an unusual moment of decisiveness. Of course, that was how anyone responded to a situation with no apparent choices. You pay the IRS, you show up to funerals, you understand the seriousness of a transplant.

In a way, making the purchase of the blasted airline ticket made the decision a concrete reality. He had a piece of paper in his hand, an itinerary, and a credit card transaction record. No choice. You don't blow off airline reservations, either. As soon as he'd heard the word— transplant—he'd gotten on the Internet. He'd sealed the deal.

The consequences Arturo's leaving could have on their relationship were frightening. Both Joe and Arturo doubted he'd be granted another tourist visa, not without the all-important paperwork the American consulate would demand. It would leave them in another situation with gravely few options—Arturo would stay in Guanajuato or he would cross illegally. Joe had no suspicions about Arturo's intentions—their relationship and business were at a peak. His only concern was for Arturo's ability to carry out his intentions.

Despite the possible obstacles, Joe would never be the person who kept Arturo from being at his mother's side during the procedure, and perhaps from seeing his mother one last time. Joe knew Arturo had not been present for the passing of either of his grandparents, an unfortunate fact that Arturo had never entirely gotten over. Had Joe left it up to Arturo to make the decision whether or not to return to Guanajuato, the man might have wavered. Maybe some of Arturo's Catholicism had finally rubbed off on Joe—making the ultimate sacrifice was clearly the right thing to do.

He'd had an unsettling sensation the day Arturo left. But he always had unsettling sensations when it came to big decisions, especially those that went against his selfish impulses. The day Arturo had left proceeded like most any other day. Joe went to the restaurant and worked with automaticity. He hadn't eaten anything that day, but he had no appetite, the emotional emptiness paradoxically taking up all the space inside him. When he did eat the next day, his actions were again automatic, like putting money in a payment machine.

When he had called Arturo that first night, he had imagined his partner in a hospital surrounded by solemn faces. He pictured the narrow, hilly streets, and the cobblestones. He saw the tall gray and brown buildings with tall doors and thick metal knockers. The packed streets of the Festival Cervantino were barren in his mind, a single, faceless person walking by. He'd heard a hint of joy in Arturo's voice, as if his own voice was an escape for Arturo, an instant return to their happy home. The joy changed Joe's vision of Guanajuato—it put children in the streets and sunshine poured in between the houses.

They would speak frequently, almost daily, until the phone calls became a nightly fixture in the routine, like imbibing a nightcap.

The first week or so was most intense, with the long days of waiting for news about Arturo's mother and whether or not her body had accepted the replacement part. She was mostly asleep or otherwise unconscious, the machines reporting any anomaly. In a room down the hall, Miriam's recovery was more troubled. She tended to toss and turn, and had bouts of delirious wakefulness. Arturo told Joe that her face would often crunch up into angry expressions and she would curse vile strings of vulgarity during sweaty, delusional dreams. He supposed any donor might have mixed feelings, albeit repressed ones.

After a couple of weeks, both mother and daughter pulled out of their stupors. The phone calls between Joe and Arturo continued. Joe had deferred to Arturo and his family's needs, pushing aside his own insecurities and wishes. As it became apparent both women would fully recover, he asked about Arturo's visa, and whether or not his lover had applied. "Pretty soon," he answered. "First I need the passport."

Days turned into weeks, and weeks turned into a month, until the phone calls, like the ones Arturo had made to his family before he had left, could no longer substitute for physical presence. Joe needed Arturo back and started to find it difficult to hold off his depression. They had spent so much time and energy to construct a life together in San Francisco, and the whole thing had been pushed to the side. His will to fight had begun to erode. His ability to maintain their routine began to diminish. He no longer stocked the pantry at home with Mexican sweet bread. He no longer kept to his side of the bed. He stored the shot glasses in the back of the cupboards.

Joe sometimes stopped and imagined what Arturo was doing. He could be such a patient man, and a single-minded one. He probably dedicated all of his time to his family, with little energy spent on how he'd return to San Francisco. In truth, Joe suspected Arturo considered the visa application with dread. Joe did. They had discussed the unlikelihood of its approval. Joe preferred to get the process out of the way—to know. Arturo seemed to want to put it off. Joe hoped at least he was putting together papers, phony though they might have been.

Joe rolled down the window of the taxi. He needed air. He hadn't thought Chava's leaving would bring up all these memories… and fears. He should have known better. Many of the feelings had been buried, but some not as deeply as others. And though Chava had not been exactly a replacement for Arturo, the similarities in their situations— leaving for an undetermined time to take care of family issues— unearthed those emotions that simmered below the surface. *This situation*, he tried to remind himself, *does not have to end up the same as the last one.*

Despite having learned to cope with the absence of a loved one, he felt the same emptiness when he returned to the restaurant, mindlessly taking orders and phone calls, wiping tables and precooking.

"You look haggard again, Joe," Alberto said as he stuffed spinach leaves into his mouth.

"Fuck you," Joe answered in a tranquil tone.

"Whoa. Take it easy, just trying to make small talk."

"Oh, sorry. It just slipped out." Joe's eyes met Alberto's for a split second before they turned back down to the table. "I'm preoccupied."

"Hey, what say we go to the park again?"

"Nah, I don't think so."

"Come on. Tomorrow's Sunday. Didn't you always go to the park on Sundays?"

"Yeah, with Arturo. We used to go skate."

"Fine, then bring your skates with you."

"Are you going to skate too?" Joe answered with a satisfying, sarcastic smile.

"No. But you can go ahead. I'll walk and we can catch up to each other."

"I've got to watch the restaurant."

"We've been through this a hundred times. They always take care of the place. We can go early; you'll be here by lunch. Joe, it will do you some good."

Alberto's concern and pleading felt good, as if someone left in the world still cared about him. Anyway, he knew Alberto was right... again... and that he should get out into the world and not let loneliness consume him. With slumped shoulders and a meager grin, he conceded.

LATE October brought cooler weather and fewer people to the park. Joe stuck beside Alberto, who sported a dark-gray pair of sweats this time, which made him look like a rhinoceros. In skates, Joe towered over Alberto. They were a perfectly mismatched pair.

Joe took in the familiarity of John F. Kennedy Drive. The wide road was open space, like a savannah on safari. He imagined the rhinoceros chasing after a Jeep and smiled to himself.

"What? See something you like?" Alberto asked.

"No, nothing." Alberto would retort with a giraffe joke if he said anything, so Joe decided to keep his mouth shut.

They proceeded without talking, Joe enjoying the breeze from the sea in his hair. He could be a seagull, riding the easy currents above the crashing surf. He closed his eyes for a moment to concentrate on the feel of the wind on his face. It let him forget.

"Go, Joe. Go ahead. I'll catch up with you."

Joe didn't wait for another invitation. He bent his knees and started striding from side to side, faster and faster, left foot then right.

He slalomed past walkers and slower skaters, kids on bikes with training wheels, and a girl on a skateboard. He left them all behind. Near the barriers, where the road reopened to traffic, Joe stopped with a graceful spin. He'd questioned his skating skills but happily found them to be as oiled as ever. He turned to look for the rhino down the road and saw a blurry gray dot. Alberto would take a while to catch up.

To the left, a large meadow hosted another group of people the wind brought with it—the kite pilots. Already couples and families sat in the grass watching a dozen kites or so maneuvering high in the sky. Two or three were big, boxy types, a few others were fancy falcons, and the rest were old-fashioned diamonds with cross-shaped skeletons. Joe rolled to the grass then stepped on it, his wheels sinking slightly into the moist sod. He found an empty patch where he could sit alone.

He decided to lie back and watch the fast-moving kites on a canvas of blue sky and slow-moving clouds. The shapes raced around like the Red Baron, the falcons hunting, the boxes hovering. A pointy bird with a long plastic tail slammed into a colored box, their strings became entwined, and down they came like wounded warplanes. Joe followed them as they got bigger and bigger and finally crashed a few feet away in a mound of ripped canvas and snapped sticks.

Two pilots ran over to salvage the wreck. They spent a couple minutes untangling before the bird's owner, a chubby kid of middle school age, apologized and ran off with what was left of his flyer. The other guy, a middle-aged man whose skin appeared browned by the sun, shook his head and laughed it off. He looked over at Joe. "It's all good," he said with a smile. "Part and parcel. Besides, I can still patch it up. This one's lasted me forever."

Joe answered with a polite nod.

"You kite?" the man asked, approaching Joe with the bright prism hoisted between his arms.

"No... just came to skate." The guy's eyes were as green as the grass, his dimples disarming.

"You should try it sometime. It gets your mind off things."

"In that case, maybe I will," Joe said.

The guy set down the contraption. "Haven't I seen you on Castro Street?"

"I doubt it. I don't get out that much. Maybe over at José Arturo Amor."

"Ah... *comida mexicana*, right?" The man's gringo accent reminded Joe of himself about six years back.

"Right."

"Good food. I'm Rick, by the way." He stretched his hand for a shake. "Nice skates."

"Thanks."

"Whoo... made it!" Joe looked to the left to find that sweaty Alberto had caught up.

"Oh, are you two...."

"No, Rick. I'm Joe, and this is my friend, Alberto. Just friends."

"Very well."

"Um... I've got to be going but... maybe I'll see you here again," Joe said, pushing Alberto toward the blacktop.

Once out of earshot of Rick, Alberto laughed like a mischievous child. "Oh... José and Ricardo. I never thought you'd finally meet—"

"Shut up, Alberto. Let's get out of here. I'm gonna be late."

Joe pulled him back to JFK Drive, and they headed to the Mission. Joe hadn't said much, feeling like a snake in a new skin. In a way, he felt elated and, in another, he felt guilty. The park had been his and Arturo's place. It did feel nice to meet somebody, but was it time?

TWENTY-EIGHT

MAMÁ and Miriam both came home after two weeks in the hospital. Though the threat of Mamá's body rejecting the organ persisted, and infection in either of them continued to be a risk, the doctors and my family agreed they'd be better off at home, where they could rest more peacefully. Besides, I'd be there to attend to them night and day, and the hospital bills were adding up. You told me over every phone call not to worry about the money, and the entire procedure cost a fraction of what it would have in the United States. We tried to economize nonetheless.

We converted the living room into a medical ward, the two borrowed hospital beds taking so much space that we had to upend the sofa and stand it in a corner. When I had heard Miriam would be the donor, I had felt a certain relief, but also a pang of jealousy. I hadn't been asked, nor had I been tested for a possible match to Mamá. My chance at dutifulness had been usurped. I secretly wondered how I would have felt had I been asked and had I been a match. A body lives well enough with a single kidney. In a sense, we all carry an extra, like a car's spare tire. But nobody recommends giving away your spare tire and driving around without one.

When they were in the hospital, I had felt like a spare tire. Long before the transplant, I had discussed going back to Guanajuato with Mamá, and we had agreed it best for me to stay in San Francisco for precisely the reason that, aside from being there, I wouldn't have much to do. With the two women incapacitated in the house, I could compensate for any prior uselessness or lack of duty. I became the chef, the house cleaner, and the nurse to both of them. They were both in delicate condition, and required cleanliness to the point of sterility, a difficult task to achieve and maintain in an old home whose front door was two meters from the street. They also required bathing and moving, feeding and careful dosing of medication, and, at times, entertainment. The television sufficed for some of that, and we'd have occasional chats before tiredness took over and they went back to sleep.

During those times, it became difficult to maintain the nightly phone calls with you. Sometimes I had to cut it short. Other times I couldn't talk at all. And with all the work I had to do, I lost the sensation that had been sticking to me like a Post-it note that I belonged elsewhere. For those first two weeks, I had felt like a visitor in my childhood home. With them in the house, I felt indispensable. My papá continued to work. It gave him something to do, and fulfilled his own sense of duty. Besides, at his age and with his mindset, he couldn't have handled my work even if he wanted to.

When their strength began to improve, you started asking me about the visa application. I thought you never understood how busy I was or how much they were counting on me. The passport and visa had taken a backseat. I would get to it, I knew. I also feared it, and avoided the pending rejection. The passport would be the easy part—Mexico surely had no reason to keep me from traveling. The visa from the US would be the obstacle. I had neither the paperwork I'd need to prove my livelihood in Mexico nor any connections to get me falsified documents. I wanted to go home to you eventually and I was afraid I simply wouldn't be allowed to.

If only you knew how much I talked about you, or how frequently I had you in my thoughts. "Joe says green vegetables are the best." "Joe taught me how to skate." "Joe this… Joe that." At times I tempered myself. I sounded like a mother talking about her newborn. I'd never get sick of your name, though I thought they might. Actually, when I listened to my own stories and hearing the extent to which you had penetrated my life, it was a pleasant discovery. Being next to you all the time, I hadn't seen how much you were inside me.

I went on about the restaurant, Alberto, Chava, and Señora Darina. I told them about the parties we hosted there. I told them about the customers we hated. It seemed like I could never stop talking about the splendor of San Francisco—all the sights to see, the mix of people, the skyscrapers, the parades and street fairs, the Golden Gate Bridge, and, of course, Joe, Joe, Joe.

Some things about you I kept to myself. I watched Miriam listen to music on her Walkman and recalled the way you would sing to yourself with your headphones on, with your screechy voice. You had no idea how awful you sounded, but there was a sweetness about listening to you, being the one to know your horrendous voice, and living with you in a place where we had no shame.

I'm sure Mamá knew, and Miriam too, but after all those years I'd been in San Francisco, and all the phone calls, and now the hospital bed chats, I had never said, "I'm homosexual" or "We're gay. We're partners." The necessity seemed not to exist. Nobody seemed to care. They liked to hear about you and San Francisco. There seemed to be no distaste about it, and they never expressed anything unusual about the situation. And they never asked me about women. As they say, "What can be seen need not be said."

You always battled with yourself about it. You gringos always ask if someone has come out of the closet. Have you proclaimed your homosexuality to the world? And then the questions about reactions—family reactions, friends, coworkers. Did they kick you out? Do they hate you? Did they send you to counseling? Do they want to fire you? Are you going to kill yourself? Or maybe they'll just ask you to take on a decorating project.

Mamá might have said she didn't understand homosexuality. She might have said the church is opposed. But if I never burst the bubble, she wouldn't have to say anything, and we could all talk about you and me and no one would have to be dogmatic or hypocritical. Instead, their implicit acceptance fit cozily under the covers.

All that talk about Joe had an unstated purpose. As their health returned, I was building them up, and building myself up also, to accept that at some point it would be time for me to go home. I managed to get an appointment for the passport. I went early one morning and got the paperwork in. A week or two later I'd go back for the new green booklet.

Mamá stood up on her own before Miriam did. I had been putting the finishing touches on a vegetable beef soup. I walked in with her tray and found her with a broom in her hand! I nearly dropped the tray right there and I promptly scolded her. "I'll get it! I'll get it!" I insisted. She reluctantly sat back down, telling me she'd seen some dust on the floor, and that I didn't have to do everything. I set the tray over her legs. Miriam had managed to stay asleep.

Mamá spoke a phrase then, quietly, in that tone mothers have that is both pointed and affectionate. "You're still my boy hero." I looked into her eyes, her irises lustrous despite the aging lids. I smiled at her and she held my hand, surprising me with the firmness of her grip. "Pretty soon, we'll have to get up and do things ourselves."

"Why, Mamá?" I wasn't sure what she meant or what the hurry was.

"Because Joe needs you at least as much as we do."

ONE day Mamá showed me her drawer of papers—bills and receipts for the house, not neatly filed like yours, but kept in a way that showed there had been little use for them. I spent a few hours one afternoon sifting through them and organizing them by type and date. Some were over ten years old, and in the sequence of them, there were often months missing. The house always had electricity and water, so the bills must have been paid. Unfortunately, I didn't believe any of the documents would be useful to me. All I could say to the Americans was that I lived and worked with my parents and all the bills were in my papá's name.

I stalled a couple weeks more until I could pick up the passport, hoping for some opportunity or miracle that would guarantee the visa. None came. I finally went down to the cybercafé and struggled my way through the US Department of State website to get my online forms filled out and request an appointment. I answered the final questions for the Americans: no, I didn't have infectious leprosy or any other communicable disease; no, I did not intend to engage in prostitution in the United States; no, I had never been involved in or been accused of committing genocide; and no, I wasn't a spy. I also answered no to the question pertaining to my intention to work there. I had no qualms about lying. They should have asked if their marriage laws discriminated against my sexual orientation. I hit submit, paid $160 with your credit card, and got my appointment. The earliest available timeslot was a month off, so you would have to fend for yourself for at least a while longer, which ensured my continued help for Mamá and Miriam.

The pieces for my return to you began to fall into place. With the application request, my yearning for you surfaced. I knew this time with my family was temporary. Perhaps I didn't always show it, but I always knew where I belonged. I had no idea I'd never get there and that my time with you was also temporary, more temporary than I had ever suspected.

TWENTY-NINE

"MEXICAN Casino Terror: 53 Dead." Joe had quick eyes for any story relating to Mexico. Over the past seven years, he had seen the reputation of Mexico change from one of a lighthearted resort destination to one of relentless drug-cartel turf wars and terrorism. In this case, during broad daylight, seven or eight unmasked men pulled up to a casino in the northern city of Monterrey. They rushed in carrying cans of gasoline, ordered the people out, and lit the place on fire. Not everyone obeyed their commands to get out. And some people ran to the back of the building, where there was no escape. Two minutes later, the place was an inferno. Fire crews discovered the majority of the victims crammed together in the bathrooms, charred and unrecognizable, with cellular phones in their hands. Joe could only imagine the urgent calls they'd made, and their final messages, and the desperation they felt as they tried to find an exit through the black smoke. They must have struggled to live. They had walked into the place on a normal day in their lives, and a few minutes later their lives had been grotesquely taken from them. An unthinkable stain for the country. No wonder people were afraid to go to Mexico anymore.

Joe refolded the paper and put it under his arm to take to the restaurant. Halloween—always unpredictable. The witches were sure to come out tonight. Not for Joe—he planned on hanging around the restaurant until closing time, or maybe he'd go home and pass out candy from his doorstep if customers didn't materialize.

He headed toward the stairs but stopped first in front of the *ofrenda*. Mexican violence. Joe often wondered if Arturo had become one of the more than forty thousand victims of the drug war in Mexico. In his worst moments, he feared Arturo had been captured and tortured.

For the first year, Joe had clung to the hope Arturo was still alive. Arturo might have been injured, enslaved, or imprisoned. He waited for a phone call, an e-mail, or a postcard. Silence. Arturo would have found a way to communicate and let Joe or his family know something. He had to be dead.

One time during that first year, Arturo's old friends, Chuy and Chepa, had come by the restaurant looking for him. Joe had met them on only a few occasions and felt a measure of contempt for them. Arturo had chosen to hang out with them and found some escape with them. Joe didn't have to like them. After he and Joe opened the restaurant, Arturo had spent less and less time with them. Once in a while, they still had their party nights. Joe explained to them the general situation, withholding the details. "Nah, maybe he didn't feel like coming back," one insinuated.

"He could have shacked up anywhere, got a better offer," said the other.

They only reinforced Joe's contempt. Obviously, Arturo had been nothing more than a drinking buddy, if they knew him so superficially. Joe excused himself impolitely from them, finding some chores to do. Few people had provoked in Joe such a profound urge to swing his hand and slap their faces. He could almost feel the gratifying sting on his palm of a double slap. He hadn't seen or heard from them since.

Of all the possibilities that had run through Joe's head, he never once seriously doubted Arturo's intentions. They say you never really know a person. Of course, there was always more to find out. But you can know a person enough. Arturo was a mama's boy, not a swindler. He wore his emotions on his sleeve. He could be impulsive, but not indecisive. When he set his mind on something, he did it. He'd had his mind set on coming home.

Joe took in the entire *ofrenda*—the photo in the center on top of the striped and colorful serape, the crepe paper butterflies, the terra-cotta dishes with olives and stale sweet bread, the flowers, the blue and white sugar *calavera*, and the motorcycle. He focused on the picture at Mirror Lake, their two faces beaming with accomplishment. Arturo's smile showed his relaxed bliss. His extended arm held the camera while the other was firmly wrapped around Joe's shoulder. Behind them, the surroundings were so perfectly reflected on the lake that it appeared as if the mountains and the sky existed in two places. Sometimes he thought that if he had only known this *ofrenda* would now be made in Arturo's memory, he would have found a way to value each day they'd had together, and to appreciate them even more. But no, one can do little more than live each moment as it comes, without regret.

Arturo used to make fun of Joe for always seeing both sides of everything, and getting stuck somewhere between the two. Arturo had a point. And now Joe asked himself if enough was enough. Perhaps the mourning period was over. Was it time to move on from Arturo?

He picked up the postcard from his mother. *It must be hard to lose someone you love.*

"Damn, Arturo."

He set the postcard back on the *ofrenda* and walked down the stairs.

"LONG face today?" Alberto asked as Joe set a sizzling platter of vegetable fajitas in front of him. "Or just part of your Halloween costume?"

"No costume for me this year."

"What? No drag either?"

Joe frowned. "Nope. Seems like a good day to wallow."

"It happens."

"And you? Going out to the Castro tonight?"

"Honey, I haven't been out on Halloween since I was a kid."

"Good—two miserable, lonely lumps in San Francisco," Joe chimed, wiping his hand on his apron and disappearing into the kitchen.

When he came back to clear Alberto's plate, the big man said, "Joe, you miserable lump. Why don't I drop by tonight and we can be miserable together. You get the candy for the kids and I'll get a six-pack."

Joe had been playing hard to get with Alberto for the longest time. Every time Alberto suggested something, Joe would resist, only to give in after Alberto's insistence. He did enjoy Alberto's company—anyone's company—so he decided to make it easy and agree to Alberto's suggestion. It seemed the restaurant would be slow. After all, it was a Tuesday, so he'd be able to get away.

At twilight, Alberto buzzed the door with not a six- but a twelve-pack in his hands. "Well, it's light beer," he said. The man labored his way up the stairs, the poor things complaining with straining creaks. On his way into the kitchen, he stopped in front of the *ofrenda*. "So this is it, huh?"

Joe nodded.

"Good picture of you two." He opened the carton of beer and set one on the table. "Have a brewsky, Arturo. We miss you."

"So, you're gonna run up and down the stairs to pass out candy?" Joe said as he lifted a huge bag of assorted taffy.

"I don't think so. Shall we just sit down there and wait?"

"Sounds like a party, but I'm not sure we'll get that many customers."

"I don't know. Make a decision."

"Always a decision to make. Can't we leave it to fate?"

"I can tell you I won't be hiking up and down the stairs. I'm liable to crush a goblin when I tumble down."

Tap, tap, tap. Both of them looked toward the stairs. Another rap on the glass of the door.

"Speak of the devil," Alberto said. "They're starting early. Guess you better take down those taffies. I'll pop you a beer."

As Joe walked down the stairs, he expected to see a group of short folk in store-bought costumes. Instead, he made out a single figure behind the curtain. He grabbed a handful of taffy and opened the door.

A young man stood there with a grin on his face and a bag at his side.

"Chava! You're back already?"

"You didn't think I was going to miss the best holiday of the year, did you?"

"I… I…."

"Well, I wasn't. Are you all by yourself?"

"Alberto's upstairs."

"*Al Puerco?*"

"Shut up," Joe whispered before reverting to his normal voice. "Tell me what happened."

"Sure. I'll tell you the whole story while we get ready for the Castro."

"You're crazy. We're staying home tonight."

"Don't be such pathetic queens. I'm not asking… you're getting dressed."

Joe shrugged and followed Chava upstairs. It was good to have some youthfulness around. "Hey, where are your keys?"

"I don't know… in my bag some place."

"Oh. You want some candy?"

Chava took the colored goodies and strutted noiselessly up the stairs.

THIRTY

BY THE time the appointment for the visa renewal came around, both Mamá and Miriam were up, slowly reentering their normal lives. Mamá even offered to accompany me to the consulate, but I felt it was something I had to face on my own. Anyway, you were there with me, holding my hand in one sense, and pushing me from behind in another.

The process went differently than I expected. A few people in town had mentioned that their renewal appointments were relatively painless. If the United States trusted you the first time, they said, by giving you the visa for ten years, then unless you got arrested or caught working, they'd have no reason to reject your application. They gave me a bit of hope, though those people had employment in Guanajuato, and the documents to back it up. And there were still more stories of the coldness of the consulate workers, the way they'd judge you in an instant, summing you up without another blink—a third-world citizen. In a word, poor.

The worker I stood in front of, a thick green sheet of bulletproof glass between us, seemed to be a compatriot. Her Mexican Spanish was perfect in a Mexico City, upper-class drawl. She went thoroughly over the few documents I had brought—my expired visa card, my birth certificate, and all the paperwork I could come up with concerning my parents' house. As she started asking questions, the look on her face seemed to be of genuine concern. I couldn't quite tell if she felt for me and wanted to give me the visa, hoping to find a way to grant the petition, or if her concern fell on the side of the United States and her job as a gatekeeper to block yet another illegal from US job opportunities. She didn't know her true power was over my marriage.

"You live in Guanajuato, then, with your family?"

"Yes."

"And you've been working?"

"Yes, I work with my papá. I get paid in cash, so I'm not on social security."

"And you've been to the United States?"

"Yes, I spent a little time in Phoenix and San Francisco."

"Did you ever work there?"

"No. Never."

"And you paid for your trip with the earnings from your job with your father?"

"Correct."

"Bank account?"

"I let my parents handle the money. It's their house. They pay the bills."

"And that's why you have none in your name?"

"Correct."

She exhaled hard and scratched her brow. "I see there is no record of any violation you committed in the United States."

I nodded. I rubbed my damp fingers against my palms below the counter. I thought I might get lucky.

"Here's the thing, Mr. García. Can you provide me any evidence that will convince me you are tied here, that you will not simply go to the United States and work there? Aside from a clean record, you're not showing me much."

"Miss," I said, "and thank you for your patience and diligence in this matter. Of course I won't work in the United States. My family is here. My mother just had surgery and she needs my help."

"Well, then, you won't be wanting to take a vacation in the United States for a while," she said. I watched as her hand wandered, seemingly on its own, to a drawer to the right of her desk from which she pulled a clunky stamp. She spoke as she lifted it. "Get a decent-paying job with social security medical benefits. Get at least six months of paycheck stubs. Go down to the bank and open an account. And, preferably, buy a property in your name." The stamp hit the crimson inkpad hard and then my application even harder. "Denied" in stoplight red.

I swallowed hard and gave her a curt thank-you. The process had been different than I had expected, but the final outcome had not.

Returning to Guanajuato from Phoenix was a beautiful homecoming. This time had been different. As much as I loved my hometown, my feelings about it had drastically changed. Employment issues remained the same—Guanajuato had little industry, mostly catering to tourists. Some businesses only opened for the weeks around the Cervantino Festival. Still, I knew I could always have a home there and we'd always find a way to make ends meet. But you weren't there. Guanajuato had become my family's home, not mine.

Mamá and Miriam's improving health had become my permit to return to San Francisco despite the visa denial. The less they needed me, the more I needed you. You had become my life. I would return to you one way or another.

THE walk to the bus terminal across town took me nearly an hour as I strolled through the old alleys of my youth, hands in my pockets, feeling a mix of nostalgia and melancholy. Little had changed in Guanajuato over the years. I couldn't help but be transported to a time when I had seen everything from about a foot lower. I felt the same wonderment I had as a child, imagining what was behind all the walls I had passed, and what had been there in years past. Still, I felt out of place, like I did when, as a middleschooler, I went back to primary school and knew I just didn't belong there anymore.

I chose a bus ride over an airplane trip. I wasn't sure why at the time. Somehow I figured taking the bus from in town would save a half-hour taxi ride, though the bus would take thirty hours and the airplane not even three. Actually, I looked forward to the time alone. I wanted to look out the windows at the passing terrain, not from way up high from where I could see the whole world, but on street level, where cars and buildings and people were actual size. I wanted to witness the reality of the place I was leaving—the vendors on the highway, the choking smoke from exhaust pipes, a fallen tree, the toiling. And I wanted to prepare myself for my arrival at the frontier whose fence would be daunting like Half Dome in Yosemite, and I there to take it on like a mountain climber. A mountain climber readies his psyche for months or years. I would have thirty hours.

With ticket in hand, I returned to my family's home. I called you right away. "José," I said, "I'm coming home. I'll be there in a few days."

You offered to come down to the border and pick me up someplace. Where, neither of us knew. Perhaps out in the desert or on some patch of highway next to a road sign or mile marker. I pictured myself like the classic statuette of a Mexican guy napping against a cactus with his sombrero tilted over his face. Then I thought of scorpions and anthills, cactus spines and border patrol agents who I didn't think would be quite as friendly as the one out in Arizona who refueled me and pushed me along my way.

That night, my last night, Mamá fried a pair of chickens someone had given us for some work my papá had done for them. I watched as she grabbed them with bare hands on our little patio outside, catching them the way an indigenous person could seemingly walk over to a river and pluck out a fish. One at a time, she swung them around by the neck as if cranking up one of those old-time cars. I thought of her kidney and wanted her to go back and lie down, but she handled the task easily. She plucked the feathers with a vengeance. It must have made her feel capable after so many days bedridden. "Easy on the fat and salt," the doctor had told her, and I watched as she covered the pieces with flour and spices and lowered them into a frying pan full of oil. You would have had a heart attack right there, amor. After that, she fried the rice before she put it to boil, and pulled from the refrigerator tortillas made of flour and lard. The food was delicious. It made me think again about staying just to save my mother from herself. I didn't think Mamá would ever change, though. Saving you and me was more likely.

My papá and I shared a couple shots of tequila later that night. In the morning, he gave me a hug and wished me luck before he left to work, as if I had a test or a big soccer game at school that day. Mamá, forcefully back in her motherly role, made me some eggs with chorizo and a side of refried beans. It made me long for the restaurant for a moment, but I knew I'd be back to my cooking position soon enough, so I tried to stay focused on the last minutes with my family.

She was unusually quiet that morning. Actually, she'd been relatively quiet for the entire time I'd been there, due to her health. Her quietness this time had nothing to do with her kidneys. I could see the twitches near her eyes that belied her calmness. I understood. I hadn't seen her for more than four years. I had the same sadness as she, but happiness too.

Anyway, we washed the dishes and then the time rolled around for me to leave. I gave Miriam a hug first and headed for the door. Mamá stood blockading it. She reached up to grab my face between her palms, her tears breaking through the dam. She hugged me tight but spoke no words. She finally let go. "My boy hero," she said, and she crossed me. "May God protect my son."

She did not wail. Her cry was another of the sentimental ones that used to make us laugh. This time, her cry yanked my emotions up to where they got caught in my throat. I thought I might cry like she always had if I said anything, so I simply hugged her tight. I'm sure the look on my face said everything I might have shabbily attempted to express with words.

I left, and Mamá stood in the doorframe as I walked down the street. The road curved, and as I was about to lose sight of her I stopped, smiled one last time, and waved good-bye. I wiped a single tear off each cheek once I rounded the bend.

Forty-five minutes later, I reclined in the back of a Mercedes bus as its motor hummed, pulling out of the Guanajuato bus terminal headed to the north.

THIRTY-ONE

LESS than two hours after Chava's arrival, the two fuddy-duddies had been converted into Halloween revelers, Castro Street-style. A plain white bed sheet had become a toga for Alberto, who also bore a wreath of potpourri leaves, a pair of Arturo's sandals from somewhere in the back of Joe's closet, and makeup a la Julius Caesar at his campiest. For Joe, Chava put together a samba outfit from a length of red velvet, complete with a headdress of fresh fruit. Then Chava turned the focus to his own costume while Joe and Alberto alternated in periodic trips down the stairs for trick-or-treaters.

When Chava took off his shirt to try on a bra, Joe saw a piece of gauze the size of an index card taped to his shoulder. Joe hadn't yet asked how things had gone in Gilroy, having dedicated all of his attention to the unexpected festivities. Given Chava's mood, it seemed things might have gone well, but his rapid return and the strip of gauze made Joe wonder.

Chava first tested some oranges from a fruit bowl in the kitchen, placing and adjusting them in the brassiere, but they made it hang down too low. So he reverted to balled-up socks. Joe stood outside the bathroom as Chava began to curl his eyelashes.

"Well, how'd it go?" Joe asked.

"Fine," Chava answered, "except the ones on the bottom are too short to curl."

"I'm not talking about your eyelashes," Joe said, growing suspicious at Chava's apparent avoidance. "How'd it go with your mother?" Joe expected to see Chava's tiger eyes. He recalled how his assumptions had led him astray with Chava the last time, and he tried to keep an open mind.

"Oh, it went fine."

"Well, what happened to you?" Joe's frustration came out in the sternness of his voice. "Did you get in a fight? Did your brother get out? And why'd you really come home so soon? I mean, you were only gone two days!"

"Relax, Joe."

"It's just that... I care. And you've been leaving me out of everything. You finally opened up the other day and now you're as closed as a virgin."

"My brother didn't get parole, okay. He got in a fight so they cancelled his hearing."

"A fight? With you?"

"No. He got in the middle of a big brawl on the cellblock. They've got the whole place on lockdown. He has to wait another year. Now, can you let me focus on my liner?" He put the eyelash curler down and twisted open an eye pencil.

"Did everything go okay with your mother?"

Chava's eyes welled up with tears. "Damn you, Joe, I'm never gonna be able to do my makeup like this."

"Obviously, something's the matter. And what's the gauze for? Can't you just tell me?"

In a fraction of a second, Chava's left hand reached over and ripped off the gauze. Joe's gaze went from Chava's impatient face to his reddened shoulder. He read the lettering across the small, round muscle, in big Old English lettering: "Amá."

"Huh?" he asked with a furled brow.

"Alright. Listen, when I got to Amá's house, she held me so tight and wouldn't let go, okay? 'My son, my son,' she kept saying." Chava lifted his sleeve to wipe his eye. "'Why weren't they all like you?' she says. And we talked all night and she told me how proud she was of me 'cause my brothers and sister are all fucked up, you know? I mean, my sister came by and she has, like, two kids now and she's really fat.

And my brothers are in jail. I didn't even see my papá at all. She says he doesn't always go there no more."

"So you got a tattoo?"

"That was something I did with an old friend I ran into. He was some dude I went to school with and he saw me. He looks way older now, unlike me. Well, beauty cream, you know?"

"And you asked him to tattoo you?"

"Yeah. I mean, he told me to go inside and have a beer. Then he said he does tattoos for this guy at a tattoo shop and asked if I wanted one. And I said okay. So he asks me what I want—a skull or a woman or a dude, he says." Chava let out a girly laugh. "And I couldn't think of anything better than 'Amá.'"

"So, you had such a great time with your mother that you branded yourself with her name?"

"Yeah."

"And then you came back the next day?"

"Kinda. I mean, I told her all about you and the restaurant and how I'm the cook and all, and she was like ready to cry. She was proud of me and all the responsibilities I have. And then I said, 'Yeah, I do have responsibilities. And I should get back to them,' because, anyway, her house is still depressing and she had to go to work too. And I didn't want to miss the best holiday of the year, so I said fuck it, I can go back to Gilroy whenever I want. And I came back."

"It sounds like it went really well."

"Yeah, it did. I mean, it's sad to see my sister like that, and their house is trashy and all. But I hadn't ever heard Amá say she was so proud of me. Like before she didn't even realize it. And I didn't have nothing to be proud of, either. Neither of us thought I'd be anything and now I'm the shiny star of the family." He blushed and smiled proudly.

"And you came back to go drag!" Joe said.

"That's right, honey, and to make sure you old geezers get out where the rest of the living are. I knew you'd be shacked up in the house. You two may as well sleep together, go straight to bed at ten o'clock at night."

"Maybe we would have."

"Not if I can help it. Now let's get *Al Puerco* and her saggy tits so we can get out of here. Put your heels on, girlfriend. We're leaving."

THE buzz down at Castro Street could be heard from blocks off as thumping music and the general rumble of voices saturated the air. Joe walked beside Chava and in front of Alberto who seemed reluctant about going, one of his man breasts and his semi-hairy chest exposed. He huffed down the sidewalk, dropping behind until his comrades would slow down for him.

"My feet are cold," Alberto said, stopping in front of a convenience store. "Why don't we stop and get some coffee?"

"You'll heat up when we get there," Chava said.

"I can't believe you have me out here in the dark of night. I work tomorrow!"

"Quit complaining, Alberto. Have a good time," Joe said.

Alberto hunched over to take in his entire outfit reflected in the plate-glass windows of the store. "I can't believe you have me out here like this. It's embarrassing. How am I supposed to have a good time? I know I'm fat, okay? We don't have to advertise it."

"So what, yo' fat?" Chava said. "I only tease you 'cause I know nobody cares. Lots of people are fat… and lots of people like fat dudes."

"I don't care if someone's fat," Alberto said quietly.

"See?" Chava said.

Alberto peered through the glass of the convenience store, apparently trying to decide if he wanted to buy something. Joe figured he was trying to gracefully change his mood.

"Okay," Alberto finally said, lifting his chin. "Let's go down there."

They walked the final block down to Castro Street, approaching the crowd as if ready to plunge into the ocean. Just then, five built guys in white navy uniforms strutted by, holding hands and dancing to the street music. Alberto turned to the others. "You know what I like most about sailors?" he asked. "They're seamen!" He put up his fat finger like Julius Caesar orating, and then pointed into the crowd. The three plunged in together, bumping and grinding against shaking hips and swaying shoulders.

They made their way up toward 17th Street, where the streetcar usually stopped at a platform beneath its overhead wires. No vehicles would pass anytime tonight. On the far side of the street, Joe watched as a band of bears huddled near parked motorcycles in front of a bar called The Den. They held large plastic cups full of beer. The one closest to them, a graying man nearly as round as Alberto, sported a toga. "Brother!" he shouted toward Alberto. "Come on over here!"

Alberto looked behind him and over at Joe and Chava, unsure the man was talking to him. Joe pushed him toward them. "Go on, big guy," he said. "Go with your clan." Alberto gleamed and walked over toward the group. The man held out a beer to him. Alberto took it and glanced contentedly at Joe for a second before he engrossed himself in conversation with his new friends.

When Joe turned back to the street, Chava was nowhere in sight. He felt a sense of déjà vu, remembering the time he'd lost track of Arturo. He recalled the way their hands had come out of the crowd and recaptured each other, almost expecting Arturo's arm to appear now from between moving bodies. He'd been lost and would finally be found. But no arm appeared, and Joe reminded himself again that Arturo was gone. He ground his teeth and frowned, wishing he could be rid of the automatic thoughts of Arturo and the constant hope for his return.

He turned again toward The Den. Now Alberto was out of sight. Chava had disappeared too. Joe stood alone in the current of the crowd, a hopeless, lonely speck in the midst of vast anonymity. He felt paralyzed there, wanting to move, or wanting to go home, yet standing frozen in place. Now he was the one who wondered how Chava had gotten him to dress up. What was he doing there?

"José!" he heard from somewhere in front of him, and he thought Chava had returned and snapped him out of his trance.

"What's up, gringo?" another voice asked. It took a moment before Joe realized he had run into Chuy and Chepa. He strained to smile, tasting the bitter flavor they always brought to his mouth.

"What are you doing?" Chepa asked. "You look like a giraffe out here by yourself. What's wrong? Still waiting for Arturo to show up?"

The tiny smile on Joe's face vanished. He couldn't believe the guy would have the gall.

"Get over him! If he finally does show up, it ain't gonna be for you, okay? He can't be dead. They go after drug runners and gangsters, not regular guys like him."

Joe's frown turned into a scowl, in part because it seemed they had read his mind—he had been waiting for Arturo. Waiting, waiting, waiting, and never able to give him up for good.

"Fuck off, you short, drunk spics!" he yelled, pushing away from them through the crowd as if swimming through thick lava. A heel gave out on him as he stepped, and he would have fallen if it hadn't been for the wall of bodies around him. He didn't want to look back, imagining their laughter.

He got home with his heels and wig in his hand, his bare feet dirty and sore, and his makeup a wreck. Worse, he had come home alone. What had started off as a fun evening out had become a reminder of good times turned sour. When he got the door open, he dropped his pumps on the landing with a hollow thud and then hiked up the stairs.

At the top of the stairs, he could see the candle flickering on the *ofrenda*. He didn't remember having lit it, and figured Alberto or Chava must have done so. The wick had burned down near the bottom and the glass had become smoky black. Joe fixed on the stale sweet bread and the few olives left in the dish. They looked as ridiculous as his wish that Arturo would someday return. The motorcycle toy sat there, mocking his past ignorance. Vroom, vroom. He imagined Chava and Arturo cruising the San Francisco hills as he worked blindly at the restaurant. They must have had a blast without him. Then he took in the butterflies. Stupid insects. *They're not so stupid that they don't know where they're headed, though.* Joe, he never knew. He didn't know where to go or what to do. He was still lost and lame without his lover, after all this time.

He imagined Arturo with somebody else right now. Would he be thinking of Joe? Would Arturo remember and feel the constant torment? Would Joe constantly mask his never-ending grief with a superficial smile? Where was he? Would the emptiness never end? Tears began to build up in his eyes, but so did the anger in his jaw and brow. "Fuck!" he screamed at the *ofrenda* in the empty house. "Fuck you! Fuck you all!"

His arms came up first to pull his hair. But then, in a single thrashing motion, they went to one side of the *ofrenda* and wiped the entire table clean. He was like a waiter gone mad. Olive oil splashed to the floor, the glass candle vase shattered, and pieces of terracotta scattered in all directions. The motorcycle drove off someplace, and the colored serape hung sadly on a corner of the table. The *calavera* landed crookedly on the floor, the jawbone separated from the rest of the skull, its eyes staring into space. Joe sat down in place, hearing the crunch of shards beneath his skirt. He didn't care. He sighed and closed his eyes, relieved by the catharsis.

When he opened his eyes again, he saw a potato beside him. He flipped over the postcard from his mother. *Count on family*, he read, before looking down at the angel wings. They were just the shape of some of the crepe paper butterfly wings. Yes, butterfly wings always knew where to fly. He turned the postcard around in his hand and decided to book a flight at once.

THIRTY-TWO

AMOR, it is okay for you to get angry. Anger liberates. Somewhere inside, you know I was always with you. And that I still am.

On the bus ride, a guy from Mazatlán sat next to me. He was about my age, but scruffier and heavier, and he said his name was Gerónimo. Like me, he was traveling by himself to the north. "I never stay in Mazatlán in October," he said. He'd been born there and grown up there, long enough to know. "Hurricanes. All the hurricanes come in October."

When he started telling me about myriad ways to cross the border, how to evade the border patrol or, worse, the bandits, I suspected he'd been running from something besides the weather. He held up four fingers that looked permanently dirty, I could only imagine from what. "One," he said, "you hire a coyote and they lead you through the hills. Sometimes they set you up, though, and lead you right to their friends who wait with guns or knives. Two, hike it yourself and take your chances. It's easier to get lost than people think, and they don't bring enough water. They don't realize it's all mountains and hills, and much farther to get from one highway to the next. Three, go through a tunnel. They're mostly used by the drug runners. The tunnel might be your grave. Or they could make you a slave and then they'll kill you afterward anyway."

Too many lines in a face his age told of countless stories, and their gravity killed any lightness to the discussion. He stared into my eyes as if trying to see if I had the guts to cross after all he had told me. "And four?" I asked him calmly.

"Four, get in the trunk of a car and cross your fingers. You have to pay the driver. And now they're checking almost all the trunks. Hardly any crooked border patrolmen left. Besides, they have these little boxes on posts over every lane. They say they X-ray the cars and can see the people in them. Used to be a sure method. Now it's a fool's way."

"What about swimming? They don't call us wetbacks for nothing."

"I don't swim. Anyway, you're not going to Texas. There's no Río Grande where you're going."

"You don't swim? Aren't you from Mazatlán?"

"I told you—I'm scared of the ocean. It brings the hurricanes."

We both fell asleep after that. He snored and grunted while I dreamed of powerful winds and dark tunnels and bad people. He probably felt powerful, planting fears in my head. I knew the border could be dangerous. I wasn't sure how true it all was, except I did know the border was just a single line. And I remembered from geometry class that a line actually takes up no space. You're either in the United States or Mexico. Nor did I have a choice, anyway. I mean, I would choose which way to cross, but whether or not to cross was not a question.

By the time we made it to Torreón, I was already tired of sitting. The seat was luxurious, not anything like you would have imagined. It reclined and had a leg rest so I could almost lie down flat. But the sunlight through the window was wearing, the noise from the scratchy television irritating and penetrating, and the long hours became dreary. I thought of you waiting for me and that kept my spirits up.

I considered taking a plane from Torreón up to Ciudad Juárez, but I needed to go west toward California, not just north to Texas. In Chihuahua, Gerónimo left from my side. He invited me to go with him, and make the "run" across the border together. He said he'd show me the way. But I had a vision of him being the one who led people to the bandits. Maybe his fingers were dirty from the filthiness inside him oozing out. *No*, I told myself, *just head toward Joe*. So I stayed on hours longer, until the bus pulled into Nogales.

The bus had two drivers. One would drive while the other took a fold-down seat in the stairway of the bus. Since they took turns, we barely stopped, except for once every five or six hours at a convenience store along the highway. It seemed the gas tank of the bus was infinite because I don't remember them ever getting any, though of course they must have. We did stop once or twice at military checkpoints. One of those times was in the middle of the night, and they made us all get out and unload our stuff, and the soldiers went through the suitcases and boxes and plastic bags one by one.

The bathroom in the back stunk. Somebody had thrown up in there. Urine ran on the floor. The toilet paper had run out. Neither of the bus drivers seemed to think it was his job to clean it. I would hold the urge for the next stop.

I felt you, amor, when we got to Nogales. We were right on the border. I caught a few glimpses of the fence and the border crossing where lines of cars fanned out into a dozen lanes of backed-up traffic inching along, and of thousands of red taillights. I wished I could have been in one of those cars with a valid visa in my hands—just waiting the one or two hours before withstanding the interrogation and then driving right on through. No, I was no longer welcome.

Once we left Nogales, we headed back south about an hour before we could turn west to Caborca and Sonoyta. I felt happy to be in Baja California, but scared too. The time to cross approached, and I hadn't yet decided on a specific plan. No matter what, it would be good to get off the bus and put my buttocks back to work. I feared I had flattened them. And maybe they'd carry me over the line easily, and I'd crawl into bed with you before either of us even noticed I'd been gone.

The desert encompassed parts of the states of Chihuahua, Sonora, and Baja California, and extended across the border into Arizona and California. I caught glimpses of its expansive flatlands stretching to the northern horizon, and I remembered those days and nights of free flight at eighty miles per hour. If only I could have had that motorcycle to fly across then.

As we moved westward and traveled parallel to the border, I wondered if I should get off in some arbitrary place. The border fence at this stretch was made of wooden barricades like the kind you see in

World War II movies that were meant to keep the landing craft off the beaches. The tall fence was still limited to the more populated regions. And people generally knew the true obstacle here was not the man-made barricade but the mountain range. My palms started sweating. At one point, I was ready to ask the driver to let me out. I thought to myself that for a hundred pesos he would stop the bus in the middle of nowhere. But then I saw a small group of border patrolmen on ATVs scurrying through the hills like fleas on a dog and I decided against it. Sooner or later, I'd have to make a decision.

It was just a couple more hours to Tijuana, where I had no intention of arriving. Tijuana had become one of the largest border cities partly because of the accumulation of people like me, who had intended to cross, made their way to the border, and then realized it was harder than they had thought. Either they squatted in Tijuana and stayed put or got caught somewhere along the border trying to cross it and got dumped in Tijuana the way we leave garbage on the curb for pickup. Anywhere was better than Tijuana, the Mexican melting pot, a huge urban fright. I'd rather take my chances on my own in the desert than get swallowed up like a bean in a cauldron in Tijuana.

The stretches of straight highway turned to sloping curves. The flat desert bed gave way to steep mounds of red boulders, not blood red, but the oxidized iron red of Mars. We had entered the Rumorosa, and I guessed its name came from rumors and legends about the geographic anomaly that had arisen throughout its history. It seemed God had decided to place his collection of boulders here in great mounds reaching into the sky, so high that this part of Baja California received snow in the wintertime.

Along the way, people had stopped their cars to view the scenery or take a quick whiz in the rocks. In the opposite lane, a truck had flipped, its brakes likely having given out on the down slope. Graffiti marked certain boulders, particularly large ones or those perilously perched, with lovers' marks or gang tags, or something more ominous—"They are coming" written beside a symbol of the Zapatista National Liberation Army. Martian plants sprouted from between the rocks, strange cactus shapes that stood erect in an otherwise lifeless place.

We descended the far side of the mountain and returned to lower hills and more desert. The driver announced our arrival at Tecate, the neighboring city to Tijuana, and I knew I had to get off, lest I plop myself into the big city. The town was situated at the foot of American hills, the border fence like a thick line drawn in black permanent marker along their base. A single street crowded with store signs, tacky advertising, and neon defined the town center.

I got off the bus and went into the first motel I came across, above a number of storefronts. The room cost me about fifteen dollars, its central feature a cheap mattress with an old bedspread on a metal bed frame. A plastic Tecate chair sat beside it. It had no TV or even a phone, and the water in the shower came out cold. I didn't care because I only planned to stay one night.

I had to call you. I wanted to tell you I was fine and I would see you soon. But first I wanted to know my plan for exactly how that might happen. I ventured out into the street, and at a corner stand, I got a couple carne asada tacos slathered with spicy salsa and mashed avocado, cilantro, and diced onion. It reminded me that I'd have to get enough provisions and plenty of water. Then I realized that, without thinking about it, I had been leaning toward a solitary trek through the mountains—no coyote, no drug tunnels, and no car trunks.

I wandered into a bar with a huge Tecate sign outside. I wondered if the beer had been named after the town or vice versa. And I wondered at the chance of getting a Miller Genuine Draft. I took a stool of ripped red vinyl at the bar. "Tecate?" the bartender asked me. I nodded. He'd already had the brown bottle in his hand and open for me.

"Crossing or just passing through?" a guy with a Los Angeles baseball cap asked me out of nowhere. He took a seat at the next stool.

"No, just passing through," I said, "visiting family in Tijuana."

"Okay," he said with a grin, "that's why you're in Tecate, not in Tijuana."

I shrugged.

"I got passage. Guaranteed. We take groups every day, six to ten people, that's it. You in?"

"I'm good."

"Seriously? You think you can make it out there on your own? You don't know the way. I'll bet you've never been here before. You'll get lost, you'll get hurt, you'll get killed. Anything can happen. You ought to go with someone who knows."

I didn't say anything to him, I only looked at him.

"Two thousand dollars. Guaranteed across. We have a van to pick us up, and they leave you at a trolley station in San Diego." The guy let out a hacking cough. I looked over at the bartender, whose gaze immediately veered from me. "Okay, maybe I can get you in for fifteen hundred, just for you. Single guys are easier. You'd have to help carry stuff."

I shook my head. *Just for you.* He likely said that to everyone. "I said I'm good."

"Alright. I'm telling you, they got helicopters and motion detectors and dogs. I've seen one guy get shot by a sniper. We never even saw the shooter."

I chugged down my beer, left two dollars on the bar, and walked toward the door.

"You better watch yourself," the guy said as I exited, and then, "you know where to find me. I hope you find me before they find you...."

I found a little grocery store and bought enough dry food to fill a bag—crackers, beef jerky, some candy, and apples—and two gallons of water. I wasn't sure how much I could possibly need but realized I'd be limited by how much I could carry. Water is heavy. I couldn't think of anything else I might need—I had rugged clothes and decent shoes—so I bought a phone card.

You answered right away. In my mind, I could see the hopeful glint in your eyes. You could hardly believe I was at the border, only five hundred miles away. I told you I'd be going on my own through the mountains. "Be careful," you repeated, and, "I love you." I didn't want to get too sappy, though. I felt like I needed fortitude and clarity of thought. I needed to be prepared for the elements and for danger. I couldn't be fogged by sentiment. You offered to come down for me, as if you could drive over and pick me up. I wanted to keep it uncomplicated—nobody but me confronting the powers that be. It excited my sense of adventure in a way, and made me salivate, though the danger made me swallow hard.

The credit on the phone card started running down. I watched the diminishing digits on the little public phone screen. "I've got to go, Joe."

There was a pause filled with longing and fear. I sucked it up. "Eight more pesos," I said.

"Good-bye. *Adiós.*"

"No, Joseph," I said. "I'll be there in two or tree days. I love you. I won't say good-bye, then, but *hasta luego.*"

Four pesos, two pesos, zero. The phone line went dead.

THIRTY-THREE

REASON for your visit? Joe read the question from the list of questions on the Mexican visa application, a long, narrow piece of cardstock, and an absurd contrast to the complicated American process. He was already on the plane. He'd entrusted Chava to take care of the restaurant without much explanation. He'd booked at the last minute, needing to get there before the Day of the Dead for some reason. What reason, exactly? He could hardly answer the question on the piece of paper because he wasn't sure of the answer himself. All he knew was that something suddenly called him to Guanajuato, and he decided to let the urge lead him the same way the monarchs fly, not knowing where they're going, for they'd never been, but trusting in the direction felt within. He looked at the form in the dimness of the cabin light and put a check mark on the tourist box.

He and Arturo had intended to return to Guanajuato together. Arturo had always talked a lot about it. They'd planned going in some distant future, when either gays could marry or Arturo could get his visa again, since once it had expired, traveling outside the US was impossible. Joe could travel to almost anywhere, unquestioned, yet Arturo had been trapped. They were two people with vastly different power based on where they'd been born and how much money they had. The world was a cruel place.

Arturo had told Joe countless stories of Guanajuato and his youth in the province. Joe could picture it so well he felt as if he knew the people Arturo had told him of. The days he had spent with Arturo's family during the Cervantino had always been a fond memory. Arturo's mother had behaved hospitably and generously. She'd prepared food and cleaned incessantly.

Since then, she and Joe had spoken over the phone a few times. He never called her mother-in-law and hadn't let on about his and Arturo's relationship in any direct fashion, but he sensed she knew, and Arturo had said as much. Once in a while, he wondered what she really felt. He wanted to ask her, "You know we're gay, right? What do you think about it?" Arturo droned on about cultural differences and leaving well enough alone. He explained the glories of conscious ignorance— see no evil, hear no evil, and have no need to face controversy. Joe had promised not to say anything or disrupt Arturo's way of handling it.

Now he wondered how she might receive him. He pictured her straining over to the front door, still suffering from the effects of her surgery or from age, but in his mind, he couldn't make out the expression on her face. Would she be angry? She could certainly blame him for Arturo's disappearance. After all, Arturo had left Guanajuato to be with Joe. And then she and Arturo hadn't seen each other for four years. Would she even recognize Joe? They hadn't seen each other for seven years. Would she care? She might think of him as just another tourist passing through, wondering why he'd come, since it wasn't the Cervantino.

He noticed he hadn't given a thought to Arturo's father or sister. It seemed mothers carried a heavier importance for some reason. He thought of his own family, and the postcard his mother had sent. Sure, she had considered Daddy's perspective when she wrote, worried about his temperament and opinions, but in the end she chose to send the card, bridging the gap, finally attempting to reunite, if only in a cursory way. Chava was no different. He went home for his mother, his amá, not his brothers or sister or father, just for his mother. Perhaps it was a gay thing, Joe pondered. Mothers might not always know best, but mothers always know.

Surely his mother had known too. Maybe she had suppressed it or denied it, but mothers have a sense about things. Joe had sometimes doubted the wisdom of his declaration at the restaurant that night. He had not regretted doing it, but he regretted having to lose his family over it. Had he kept it quiet and held on like Arturo had, things might have been different. To his way of thinking, he couldn't live a lie. Arturo spoke of it like a privacy issue—*who I go to bed with is of no importance to my parents*, he'd say. What Joe had always considered an issue of right or wrong boiled down to point of view. One thing his mother had written was true—it was time they spoke again.

The plane circled over San Miguel de Allende. Joe had arrived in a couple short hours. He thought of Arturo's cross-country bus ride. For some reason Arturo had chosen not to fly, perhaps, Joe thought, because of some of the same emotions knotting now in Joe's stomach. Maybe he had wanted to postpone the arrival and his inevitable confrontation with fate. Or had he needed the mental prep time? The plane touched down bumpily before the brakes heaved him forward against the seat belt, jolting his already stirring innards.

Once in the taxi and en route to Guanajuato, a settled feeling came over him. He neared a destination he'd put off for three years. When outlying homes of Guanajuato began to take the place of open space, he felt enveloped in a cozy calm, as if he had returned home, a lifeless mummy exhumed, a spirit rekindled. He breathed in the air and caught a whiff of burning wood from chimneys or firepits. The taxi passed beneath an ancient tree that held out its boughs like open arms. A pair of children stopped their play beside the road and waved at the passing car, the width of one's smile compensating for his lack of teeth. Joe rubbed his hands on the seat and noticed it was covered by a serape whose vibrant colors had faded.

"Where to?" the driver asked.

He thought of finding a hotel first, apprehensive about showing up at Arturo's house unannounced or possibly unwelcome. Yet if Arturo's family opened the door to him, how might he explain without offending them his having found lodging first?

"I'm not sure," he answered. He'd go to Arturo's house. Yes. If for nothing more than Arturo's memory. But he did not know the address. "I'll tell you as we go along."

The streets seemed deserted. He had expected stillness, the Festival Cervantino having passed already. He hadn't expected morbidity. He spotted the movement of only a few people up and down the entire length of the street. Two or three cars moseyed along, a woman stood fanning herself in the open door of a café, and an older man walked beside an elderly woman stepping slowly behind a walker.

He hardly recognized the place after so many years and without the crowds of people. Yet he felt guided too. The roads seemed less unfamiliar than he had supposed. "Take a right over the bridge," he said, "and the second left." The neighborhood became more familiar as he approached, as if he peered through Arturo's child eyes as he came home from school with Miriam beside him. He almost waited for a neighbor to step out of her door and greet him and, if he were Arturo, he might return, "Good afternoon, Señora Magdalena." And he'd hope for a cookie or a cold glass of hibiscus tea. He'd drop off his sister and go play soccer with some school friends for awhile. Or maybe he'd explore some dry river canal or a dank tunnel or see if kittens still inhabited a nook under the bridge. Then he'd have to return home for supper and for homework, for bed and school the next day.

"Three more doors down on the right," he said. The taxi stopped in front of a wooden door. He was certain he had located the correct house, though it looked smaller than he had remembered, squeezed tight between similar homes on either side. It was built up into the sky, its height disproportionate to its narrowness. The colonial-style ceilings meant to keep out the summer heat yielded tall buildings not unlike the Victorians in San Francisco in their proportion.

He fixed on the door, hoping it might open and spare him the need to knock. He pulled out his travel bag, paid the driver, and then stood on the curb, looking up at the house the way a child looks up at his father. "Here we go," he said to himself, crossing himself—something he'd never done—before stepping up to the door. He lifted a fist to knock on the door, not yet sure what he would say to her. He drew a breath.

"Can I help you?" Arturo's voice, slightly gruff. He turned to one side to see Arturo's father walking toward him. The man's face lit up. "José? What a miracle! What are you doing here?"

"Señor García." Joe held out his hand, but the man opened his arms for a hug.

"I hear you still have that gringo accent."

"I guess so, Señor García. Haven't been able to kick it yet."

"Call me Arturo." The man pushed open the unlocked door. "Now come inside and let's see what Mamá has made us to eat."

Arturo pulled a chair at the dining room table for Joe and went straight into the kitchen, yelling, "Mamá! We're hungry."

A voice came from up the stairway. "Papá, is that you? Who is *we*? Is somebody else here?" Joe couldn't decide where to put his hands as the woman made her way downstairs. "The food's on the stove," she continued. "I just laid down for a quick siesta before you got home."

Joe saw her slippered feet before he saw the rest of her. He could tell she was still recovering, and had perhaps aged a bit, as her movements seemed to take a degree of effort. When her head cleared the top of the stairwell, a smile came across her face, and she rushed as much as she could while she gripped the handrail of the stairs. "José? José? Oh my God, José!"

He stood up and met her at the bottom of the stairs. He bent over as she reached up to give him a hug that seemed to never end. It tugged at him for a moment as he wondered why his own mother's hugs had never felt this way. Finally she stepped back to look at him, wiping her cheeks with the sleeves of her sweater. "Oh, José, it's so nice to see you. And why didn't you call? You just showed up the day before Day of the...." A comprehending expression came over her face. "Ooohhh."

She pointed back to the table. "Sit down. You're with family now, so you must eat. You're skinny as ever. And then I'll take you upstairs so you can see the *ofrenda*."

THIRTY-FOUR

I HITCHED an early morning ride east in the back of a pickup truck. Three cowboys were in the front, ranch hands, I figured, on their way to work. We drove for about half an hour along the border. Where the highway turned south, they pulled onto a dirt road that continued along the border, supposedly to the ranch they worked at. I felt leery—feeling I couldn't trust anyone—even though they wore jeans and boots and looked and smelled like ranchers. They dropped me off about five miles from the highway, pointed me north, and then they drove off in the pickup in a cloud of dust.

The morning autumn air felt crisp and the clear sky promised sunshine, though I doubted it would get very hot as time and my altitude progressed. October seemed to be the perfect month for crossing—not so hot that you die immediately of dehydration and not so cold that you freeze.

I stood there alone beside the barricade along the border. On the far side, an expanse of gray hills stood before me, inviting and challenging. I took in the length of the barricade on one side, then the other. It seemed ridiculous, like the world's largest no-trespassing sign set up for me, this one person who contemplated crossing in the vastness of the desert.

When I thought of you, the restaurant we built together, our house, and the bed we shared, the motivation returned to me. I picked up the jugs of water, one in each hand, heaved my backpack up on my shoulders, and proceeded forward.

The barricade took only a minute to hurdle. As soon as I was over, I imagined having tripped a switch causing a posse of patrolmen to descend on me in their ATVs and helicopters. Nobody came. The wind made a noise in my ear. The sun stared. And I started walking. At first, I shuffled a bit, like a soldier attempting to camouflage himself by staying low or next to trees and boulders. Soon enough, I felt silly, my shoulders started to hurt from the weight of the water, and my stealthy stride had become an ordinary walk. Step after step, hour after hour.

By afternoon, I was on the summit of some hill overlooking more and more hills. I had hoped to find shade, but the search was futile, so I sat down in some dry grass. I drank water and ate some snacks, surprised I hadn't seen any life, just its traces—tire tracks, footprints, a shot-up old sign, and trash. Near my perch, ants scavenged the carcass of a rodent. Vultures circled eerily overhead. Aside from the morbidity and garbage, the place was peaceful. Had it been any other place that didn't happen to be the forbidden border zone, or had I been doing anything besides trying to cross it illegally, I might have enjoyed my little day hike. But I knew the life and death consequences I was facing, despite the moment's apparent tranquility.

By late afternoon, any notion of enjoyment had vanished. The wind picked up and the temperature fell. I walked down into the shadow of a ravine and wondered where I was. I had looked at a few maps online and I knew that Highway 8 fell relatively close and parallel to the border. How could I miss it? But now I realized how easy it would be to become lost—I could no longer tell in what direction I was traveling, save some vague idea afforded by the sun. For all I knew, I was heading more east or west instead of north. Could I have been going back south?

I had thought I'd either have been caught by now or arrived safely in San Diego after having hitchhiked a ride west on the highway. I'd figured there'd be enough empathetic Mexicans around. I had not planned on spending the night in the desert. Yet the relentless sun eventually fell and left me in the waning light. A rock fell near me. I thought I heard footsteps. And suddenly I realized what the circling vulture already knew—I was easy prey.

By nightfall, I had found a crevice on the side of a cliff in which to hide. I had eaten about half my rations and I had drunk one of the jugs of water. One side of me was stupidly relieved to be rid of the second jug while the smart side of me knew the relief could soon be my worst nightmare, assuming I made it through the night. I pulled into the crevice as far as I could to keep any of my clothes from sight. Of course, that meant I couldn't see anything below, either. My shivering soon overtook my concern about being spotted, and I pulled my knees up against my chest as I sat in the dirt and wished for deliverance.

You stumbled into my dreams that night, the same way I had seen you the first time in Guanajuato, a tall figure coming from far off, oblivious to me. You dropped into the crevice without realizing I was there. You said something about having been looking for me. And you hugged me and hugged me, laughing like a crazy chimpanzee. I felt like you had become the mountain and I a little speck inside its safety, and I knew I'd wake up the next morning.

In the morning, my eyes were sticky and crusty with dust. I heard the caw of a bird outside the crevice. I wiped my eyes and stuck my head out. There were voices—not imagined ones, but real human voices below. My head retreated reflexively, until I raised it up again by careful measures. I could make out the Spanish of a single male voice, and his words sounded jumbled. Below, I saw him, a young guy with seven or eight brown people in ragged clothes and sandals behind him, a couple and a family, it seemed. He pointed in the same direction I had been walking and motioned his hand as if directing them up and over the next hill. Then his finger went to his mouth—they'd have to be quiet. I wondered why.

I considered joining them or at least following them, but my distrust won out. He might be leading them into a death trap or into slavery. No, I'd rather avoid them and take my chances. By the time I looked again, they had disappeared. Quiet filled the canyon. Then the sound of a motor in the distance. A pair of motors like dune buggies or motorcycles. Americans. I curled up again, my eyes and ears attentive as a cat's. I wished you had stayed with me, or had come back, because I felt afraid to be alone.

It also made me think of Mamá and my papá. If she had seen me then she would have been frightened for me. She hadn't hinted at me staying in Guanajuato, though I'm sure a part of her wished I had. Strangely, not a single part of me did. What might have seemed like a choice actually was not. I had to get home to you and, if I couldn't, then I would die trying. Guanajuato had been the training ground, the place I learned to fly. My parents had been my teachers. You were my home.

I waited as the noise of the motors dissipated in the distance. Reason told me they were probably stray cops patrolling the terrain. I could stay put and sit it out. But the anxiety in me told me to get out of the crevice, where I felt isolated and with no chance of escape. I came out of the crevice, down to another ravine, and I scurried up the valley the way the little group had gone. I had managed to fit the water in my backpack so I finally had my hands free. I stayed close to the wall of the cliff, hoping to avoid the eyes of anyone watching or hunting, vultures or eagles, humans or otherwise. I hoped I wasn't far from salvation, thinking now I was on the right path behind the coyote and his pack. As I followed in their tracks, I only hoped to avoid the gringos.

I walked for ten or fifteen minutes, holding my breath. The ravine narrowed and the walls became vertical and impossible to climb no matter what might happen. Ahead stood a big tree with a large orb of green leaves. It seemed out of place. There was no water nearby. I approached the tree cautiously, since the coyote and his pack could have sought shelter there. I heard no voices and saw no movement. When I reached the tree, I saw more trash strewn about, as if someone had opened a large bag of garbage and scattered it. Blankets lay on the ground, as if someone had awakened from a slumber and run off.

Another bird flew overhead. I looked up to the top of the cliff, where I could see some rocks suddenly fall. Natural earth movement, I supposed. I tried to keep my wits about me. *Don't panic. The earth shifts, soil erodes, and rocks fall.* The sunlight was making its way over the ledge of the cliff. Another rock about the size of an apple tumbled down. Something besides gravity made it fall, I knew. I quickened my pace, hoping to find an exit from the threatening place.

"Hey!" a voice called from up above.

I should have run. I couldn't help but look up again to try to locate the source of the voice. The sunlight broke through and blinded me for an instant. Then something flew toward me from way up high. A bird, I imagined, or a rock. The next thing I knew, I was lying on the ground in a small patch of blood and shattered glass. It wasn't blue like the Corralejo bottle, or even the brown of the Tecate beer bottle, but clear glass and sharp shards right in front my face. The next instant, I realized I was lying on the ground, my cheek against the dirt. But you had known, amor. You always said the bottle would kill me.

My head throbbed. I could do little more than keep my eyes open and try to comprehend what was occurring. My pack felt strange against my back. I had fallen awkwardly and the pack seemed to pull against me. I didn't feel my legs or my arms.

I heard steps coming toward me swiftly. I had tried to evade the gringos and now my only hope was that they would return and find me and pick me up. Perhaps they'd give me water and gasoline for my motorcycle again and push me along the highway. But then a mangled tennis shoe stepped on the glass near my eyes, and I knew they weren't the shoes of a friend.

The man bent down, his scruffy face close to mine, checking if I was still alive. I shifted my eyes to see him. "Hmm," he grunted. My body moved as he pulled off my backpack. I heard the zipper and the way he chugged down the water. He pulled my things from the bag, mostly food, and hmmphed again. He dropped the bag to the ground so he could go through my pockets, back and front, while I lay helpless. Aside from my wallet, I had little to take.

I couldn't move my head anymore and I started to feel sleepy. I heard the footsteps again, this time headed away from me. I forced my eyes to open and tried to say something like "Stop!" or "Come back!" but my voice failed me. I saw the back of him and the way his elbows were up as if digging through my wallet. He'd find the picture of you and me. He'd know about us and maybe laugh. I guessed there could be worse things than someone being conscious in my last moments of the love you and I shared.

I swallowed, feeling sleepier with every second, but I fought to stay awake. I didn't want to let you down or ever let you think I hadn't tried my best to return home. "Joe." I whispered the last sound to pass my lips, like your fingerprint placed firmly on my tongue. I breathed in and out once more. Like the flame of a candle being extinguished, those eyes of mine flickered, and then closed forever.

THIRTY-FIVE

THE rest of the evening had passed in a bit of a fog. Arturo's father had pulled out a bottle of tequila, which had lubricated the bond between them and left Joe with vague memories of a long talk, laughter, and quiet, sentimental spells. Arturo's mother had refrained from drinking but not crying. Miriam had come in with her husband and child. And the small group had shared and reminisced, nurturing one another in their common loss.

Sometime in the dark of night, Joe got out of bed, Arturo's old bed, unsure of the hour. He walked into the hallway in his pajamas and was called by the candle on the *ofrenda* in the hallway. He had seen it the day before, but had not allowed himself to observe it thoroughly, or absorb it. It had called to him, but Arturo's mother had been so attentive to him that he'd felt almost captive. He wanted to take in the *ofrenda* in his own way.

Now he stood in front of it. There was no noise in the house. Joe focused on the steady burn of the candle whose flame must have stayed lit all through the night in the glass jar nearly identical to the one back in San Francisco. He raised a Ziploc baggy with the blue and white *calavera* that he'd brought from back home, pulling the two pieces from the plastic and setting them carefully on the *ofrenda*. Beside them sat a tray of little cubes of yellow cheese, edges darkened, and a small bowl of olives. The white sugar topping of stale sweet breads had started crumbling to the tablecloth. In the back, a black and white portrait of a young couple in a scratched frame leaned against the wall, beside a vase of flowers starting to wilt. The photo had seen its decades, and Joe imagined it had existed unprotected for many years. Fading had taken the lower half of it, as if it had been hung for unknown numbers of years on a wall only partly shielded from the sun. It had a crooked crease down the middle and various pinholes in the upper corners. The faces were without expression—neither frown nor smile—but the eyes still glistened after all this time.

Arturo. There he was, a small passport-size photo wedged into the frame beside the picture of his grandparents. Also black and white, it had been taken when he was a boy, about ten years old, Joe guessed. He wore a big smile and his thick, black hair was combed to one side of a profound part. He had none of his manly facial hair and his nose appeared small, but his jaw line and the shape of his eyes were unmistakable. He looked alive, as if about to say "Mamá!" or "José!" or run down the street or jump up and down or into the bed.

The flame moved. "Good morning." Arturo's mother, Señora López, had opened the door and stepped into the hallway. "You're up early."

"Really? I didn't check the time."

"Just before six."

"Okay."

"Good. We should go early to the basilica. You are coming, no?"

Joe nodded.

"Did you sleep well?"

"Yes. The room feels just like it did seven years ago."

"We left it as it was."

"It even smells the same," Joe said, hoping his comment didn't sound impolite.

She looked at him thoughtfully. "It does, doesn't it? Smells like he was just here yesterday. Or even today, right now." She closed her eyes. "I can almost hear his voice. Of course, I always feel this way on the Day of the Dead, as if all those people we lost were still right here with us." They stood in silence for a moment. "Well," she said, "I guess we should get ready and go."

An hour later, they had started walking to the basilica. Arturo's father had dutifully gone to work, leaving Joe alone with Señora López. As they approached the town center where the church was, there were more people in the street, all heading toward the great doors. Business boomed for vendors of flowers and religious paraphernalia near the front gate, as almost every person would carry a candle or a cross or a rose inside. Men chatted quietly in small circles and women wept. Oblivious little girls stood in white dresses with bright flowers, and slender boys in suits with skinny ties chased each other, a contrast to the otherwise somber mood.

Joe and Señora López joined a line of people entering the basilica. Another line exited and bent down the street in the direction of the cemetery. The church doors were conventional openings cut into the enormous portals. Joe bent down and stepped over the ancient wood doorframe. When he stood up straight, he felt a dizzying wave within him, perhaps in reaction to the dense, incense-filled air in the cathedral and the solemn mood of the people who filled it. They stepped methodically toward the aisle, dipping their hands in a bath of holy water and crossing themselves before proceeding.

Joe followed the line, which began to disintegrate as some people stepped to one side into the pews to kneel and pray, while others stood in groups or singly and whispered to themselves or to one another. As they approached the front of the church, Joe saw a grand table holding scores of lit candles. Joe had been following Señora López, but when she veered into a pew halfway up the aisle, he continued forward. Something had called to Joe. The candles. And he continued, slipping into a trance as he got closer to the altar and the looming crucifix suspended against a backdrop of stained glass. In his ears, mumbled voices dwindled to a murmur, and he stepped ever closer to the table and the candlelight.

When he finally reached it, he heard the chink of coins as people dropped donations into a velvet collection bag set at the front of the table. His head seemed to spin for a moment in the many flickering lights. But one caught his attention, a tall candle in a glass vase, whose little flame burned steadily, without flickering or dancing. He fixed on it and got lost in it as visions of Arturo began to fill his mind and the voice of Arturo hinted into his ear, "Ay, amor, you've come at last."

"Let's go now." It was the voice of Señora López. "I'm done. It's time to go." She grabbed Joe by the elbow, snapping him out of his stupor. "Time to go to the cemetery. I've got to get home to fix the food."

He almost yanked his arm from her, wanting to stay. He looked about him at all the people and didn't want to make a scene. So he followed her out the exit door, and then they followed the droves to the cemetery, where she placed flowers at her parents' grave, cried for a while, and led Joe back to the house. Though he had come to Guanajuato on his own, now he found himself in the role of a houseguest. He felt grateful for the welcome they had given him, and all the ways they doted on him. Yet he had felt interrupted in that moment and could hardly concentrate on anything but that trance under which he'd fallen, and the incompleteness of it.

In the early afternoon, Arturo's father came home for lunch. After they ate, Señora López finally lay down to sleep. Joe had his chance. He stepped out the door and headed back to the basilica.

There was more movement in the street now than earlier in the morning. A few cars drove by and people walked to and fro, but Joe hardly noticed them as he remained fixed on his destination. He drifted by stores and homes and pedestrians as if he were floating. But then, after passing a freakishly tall man, he turned and realized the man had turned around, too, the two like a pair of dogs that had recognized a scent on each another. On second inspection, the man wasn't so tall, he just had a little girl on his shoulders.

They took each other in with eyes squinted, not suspiciously, rather as if they were trying to recollect the name of a long lost schoolmate. "Don't I know you?" the man said.

"Umm... I believe so." They stepped closer. "I'm Joe."

"Ahh... Joe! José! Yes, the gabacho! I've heard of you. I don't believe we ever met, but Arturo talked about you. I'm sorry about him, you know? What can I say?"

"Right…," he said, his eyebrows raised inquisitively.

"Isaac," the man said, putting his hand out. "I'm Isaac, Arturo's old friend."

"Okay." The relief of a mystery resolved came to Joe's brow. "I should've known."

"Not really," Isaac responded. "We'd never met."

"True, true. But as you've heard about me, I've heard about you too."

"Oh." Isaac's eyes darted to the sky for a moment. "This is my daughter, Emilia. Say hello, Emilia."

The toddler chirped hello.

"Hello," Joe responded. "So… I guess you know the whole story?"

"I guess I know as much as there is to know. I had bumped into Arturo a couple times while he was here with his parents. I suppose you know that. And when he left, he'd made a phone call or two from the north and that was the end of that. Never heard from him again. What was that… about three years ago?"

"Right. He disappeared. I think somewhere in the desert in California or Baja."

"I'm so sorry. I mean, I know you guys had a thing going. And… ah… well, I'm sorry. He was a great person, a good friend."

"Yeah. I agree."

"I mean it seems like I just saw him, like we just played soccer or hiked up the hill together. You know, like he never really left. Great people don't really leave, anyway. They always stay with us for what they meant to us, or the way they changed us."

"That's right," Joe answered, beginning to feel the same trance he'd felt in the morning in the cathedral, as if spirits were churning in the air and coming up from the ground. As if Arturo were near. "Nice to meet you," he said quietly, preoccupied but not despondent. He turned and continued intently toward his original destination.

His pace quickened. He felt driven. A yearning inside him began to stir, the same yearning and desperation he had felt for three full years. It began to possess him, taking over his chest and pushing against his ribs as if trying to break out. He started trotting, passing people without noticing them, hypnotized.

The line at the basilica still reached out the door. He inserted himself toward the front of the line, focusing only on the great door in the archway of the cathedral. He needed to get inside, yet felt neither impatience nor frustration. Rather, he burned with concentration and a powerful tranquility, an assuredness that brought him closer to some precipice he had never known existed.

In a short time, he arrived once again at the altar of candles. The church was full of people. Joe stood pressed against a sturdy lady in a black shawl who elbowed him. But he refocused on that one candle still holding the steady flame and he was at once alone, as if the entire church had emptied. Yet it was different from being alone, for he was suddenly one with the whole around him. Silence descended and a single light overtook him. He became the universe.

"*Uno* means one, amor." Arturo's voice arrived inside him, not frightening like a ghost story but so naturally present, as if it were something that had been there all along, like the roots of a tree revealed or the depths of the ocean come somehow to the surface.

"Arturo?"

"You have found me."

"Where were you?"

"Here. I've been here all along."

"But you weren't. You never came home."

"I've always been home, amor. You know that."

"Are you with God?"

"You were right. There is no God, no all-powerful man. I am energy. I am the light. You couldn't see it. You couldn't open up to it or me."

"I was hurting and afraid."

"You need not be afraid. You cannot fall in empty space."

"I was afraid I lost you."

"You cannot lose me. I am you. You are me. You are tethered to all whether you are aware of it or not."

"I suffer. I hurt."

"Yes, amor. Sadness and pain and all emotion are part of the energy around us. We can only accept it and alter our perception of it."

"Alter our perception? I don't know how."

"You do, amor. You need only bend a little. You are doing it right now. Don't you see? It takes the slightest shift to convert 'nowhere' into 'now here'. Do not let fear keep you."

"And you have been here all along?"

"You expected rattling chains. I am pure presence, omnipresence, not omnipotence."

"I felt bad. I think it was my fault. I should have never let you go."

"You could only act as far as you could see. And I will not leave, though I may move over. Now is when you must let go."

"I can't forget you."

"You will never forget me. I am you. And you will again be a man open to the world, ready to share your love anew. Live."

"I love you."

"I know. I love you too. Now, love yourself so that you might love others."

"Good-bye."

"Until later, amor."

The lady's elbow bumped him again, and he regained consciousness in the midst of the church. A peaceful feeling presided inside him. He watched the candle. It burned bright and still. It seemed the others swayed with a breeze. And then, with neither smoke nor a lingering orange ember, the candle suddenly went out.

He exhaled, overcome with a sense of relief and refreshment, as if all his thoughts and feelings and instincts had reduced to one awareness. His fear and pain had been released, and he swam in the wake of their dissipation.

EPILOGUE

"YES. Reservation for twelve tonight at six under Mrs. Dickson," Chava said, his head bobbling a bit in agitation. "And by the way, I'm not a ma'am, but a dude."

Joe laughed. He knew how much Chava hated it when people got his voice confused with a woman's. In the past, he had hung up on customers over it. This time, he'd shown some control. Good thing the woman couldn't see his bobblehead.

Chava hung up the phone. "More like Mrs. Dickhead," he said to himself, jotting down the name on the pad. "Oh, hi, José! You're back already?"

"I didn't want to spend more than a few days," Joe answered. "I wasn't sure what trouble you'd get into here. Anyway, I did what I went to do."

"Trouble? You kiddin'? We got everything under control here." The young man smiled proudly. "You should have stayed longer."

Joe came in and gave the restaurant a quick once-over—through the kitchen, the walk-in freezer, the storeroom, the lobby, and the bathrooms. True, everything seemed to be in complete order. He knelt beside the shelves to check beneath them—spotless. He checked the inventory rotation in the refrigerator. The cheeses and milk products had all been properly stored in their first in, first out system. Even a new schedule for the week had been posted with Joe's name scratched out in the manager slot and another written in its place: Chava.

After checking the cleanliness of the tables and benches, Joe spoke with the prep cook and Señora Darina at the tortilla station. Everything checked out. Chava had taken care of business, they said.

Chava even had the sign out front repainted. Maybe Joe should have stayed a few more days in Guanajuato.

"Joe, can I talk to you?" Chava asked with a nervous tone.

Aha. Something terrible had happened, and all this perfection was compensation for the bad news. A health inspection, a fine, a fight, perhaps, and more detectives. Joe could only guess. When Chava pointed to the familiar corner booth for their discussion, Joe knew he would really be in for it. Then the thought occurred that if he had really screwed up, Chava might leave the restaurant, go back to Gilroy or move in with Dario again. Ugh. Or maybe something had happened at the house. He hadn't even been home yet—he had come directly to the restaurant to make sure the source of his livelihood was still intact. What was the worst that could have happened? Another bout of vandalism or, worse, Chava let Dario move in! Joe tried to relax, knowing his imagination was running away with him and reminding himself that, whatever the problem, all would be all right.

Chava scooted into the bench at the booth first. "You know, I've been here for a long time, Joe."

"Yes. A long, long time. You're thinking of leaving, aren't you?"

"Leaving? Are you crazy?"

"What is it, then?" Chava opened his mouth but Joe stopped him. "Wait, whatever it is, let me tell you the place looks great. I'm impressed. I want to recognize the good before the roof falls in."

"Thanks, dog. Come to think of it, you look pretty good too. You look relaxed."

"Now you're stalling, aren't you?"

"No, no. I just wanted to tell you that, you know, Alberto came in. He kept saying how you really needed a break and all. And I figured, yeah, you haven't taken a rest since, you know, Arturo and all...."

"Yes?"

"And so, as you can see...." He raised his hands high to indicate the entire restaurant. "I can take care of things just fine."

Joe raised his eyebrows and nodded. "Honestly, I wasn't sure you had it in ya."

"Amá even told me my jailbird brothers are jealous of me. Always have been, she said."

"Is that a fact?"

"Yup. So, anyhow, I was just gonna say, like, maybe it's time I ain't your cook and I ain't your chef no mo'."

"Are you quitting?"

"No, dumbass." Chava put his fingers up like an artist framing an imaginary picture. "Chava... Manager."

"Manager?" Joe slammed his fist on the table playfully. "Did Alberto put you up to this?"

"No, man. Anyhow, it's just a suppository. I put myself up to it. It's time to step it up a notch."

"Alright, Chava," Joe said, laughing. "Let me think about it."

"And then you can take a vacation, or at least some time off. You make enough money. Now live your life. Let me be somebody too."

Joe's extended his hand. Chava's face lit up, and his hand came out sideways, like that of a princess. "Darling," said Joe, "if you're gonna be my manager, then shake like a businessman."

Chava sat up straight and firmed up his hand. The two hands came together. "You got it, boss. You got yourself a manager." He stood up from the table and straightened his apron. "Oh, by the way," he said, after pressing his lips together, "did you go by the house yet?"

Joe shuddered. "No, why?"

"Oh, nothing. I brought you a little present, so I just wanted to see...."

"Ah. No, haven't gone yet."

"Well, don't get freaked out. It's not that big a deal."

"Am I interrupting something?" Alberto stood next to them and put his hands on their shoulders. "How'd it go, Joe?"

Joe nodded with a satisfied look on his face. "Good, Alberto. It was worth it. I got a chance to say good-bye, or *until later*, anyway."

"Fill me in later. I'm on my lunch break and I'm hungry."

"You look hungry! You must have lost, what, twenty-five pounds?" Joe's guess was genuine. Alberto's weight loss was finally becoming noticeable.

"Thirty-one, actually."

"Nice job. Keep it up." Joe walked Alberto to his usual table and waited for him to sit down. "The usual?" he asked. "Double garden salad?"

"No, my friend, this big man is back to real food. Give me a two-for-one plate, enchilada and tostada."

"Oh? No more greens?"

"I'm hanging around people at The Den who like me the way I am. I'll still lose a little weight, but I don't want to go anorexic, you know?"

"Alright, so should we make it a double?" Joe asked.

"No, just a single portion for me, thank you very much."

"Speaking of help, did you see how Chava's got this place?"

"You should have seen him taking charge around here. He's a different person."

"Things are finally coming together."

"And you can finally get some rest. What do you think you'll do?"

"Umm... I think I'll be checking out the kite field over at the park."

Joe decided to take the rest of the day off and head home to rest after his emotional week. He looked around the restaurant again before he stepped out. He noticed its flair, after all the love they'd put into it, and he smiled to himself. He waved to Chava and Alberto. "Until later."

His walk home was pleasant. He enjoyed the sights and sounds of the city. And when he stepped through the door, he wondered about Chava's surprise. At least there wasn't shit on the landing, so he had something to be thankful for. And when he went upstairs, he saw right away that not only had the *ofrenda* been picked up and put away, but the entire place was clean.

He dropped his bag in his bedroom and walked into the kitchen, marveling at the vacuumed rugs and dusted furniture. First, this home had been just his. When Arturo had come, it had become their home together. Now alone again, Joe felt tranquility in knowing that what once was could live on forever, even if he moved on in some way. Arturo was there, no matter what or whom else the future would hold.

A noise came from the kitchen. He turned his head and waited, but heard nothing else. "Hello," he said to empty space. No answer. Silly man. There'd be no slamming doors or messages scrawled on the condensation in the bathroom mirror after a hot shower. He relaxed and walked into the kitchen. On the table, there was a big box of garlic marked "Gilroy." Chava must have brought it back, a gift from his mother. Nice. One could never have too much garlic.

He heard a scurrying near the stove. He checked out the burners and observed the pilot light burning steadily. He almost expected to be elbowed. Another movement in the corner of his eye. Something dashed across the floor. He jumped up and screamed like a girl. He brought his hand to his chest to monitor his heart. A little gray kitten as scared as Joe hid beneath the table. Joe laughed and bent down to stroke it. "A pussy?" he said aloud. "You brought home a pussy?" He picked it up, a tiny toy in his hands, and he petted it till it began to purr.

Later that night, he sat at his desk with a pen in his hand. He looked at the picture on the front side of the postcard, the much-photographed tips of the towers of the Golden Gate Bridge poking out of the thick fog, a rainbow arching over it. And he wrote:

> *Dear Mom,*
>
> *Yes, it's been a long time. Glad to know that you and Dad are fine and that the old linoleum has finally been changed. I guess it's time to do some upgrades in my house too.*
>
> *Thank you for the postcard. As you imagined, it has been hard to lose my lover, but I think I am ready to move past it. Arturo was a wonderful man. You would have liked him. Since I can't bring him*

back, I can only appreciate the memory of him and all the ways he is still here with me today.

I'm not sure that we have only one family, but we do only have one chance to get things as right as they can be while we're still here on this earth.

Say hi to Daddy. Looking forward to hearing from you.

Love,

Joe

Born in San Francisco in 1970, ERIK ORRANTIA studied psychology, determined to become a therapist. When he began working as a school counselor, he found a calling in education and, later, all things Mexican. He studied in Mexico City for a year and decided to live in Tijuana to perfect his Spanish and remain immersed in the Mexican culture. He has lived there since 1998, teaching middle school in California and absorbing more about Mexico every day. He has traveled extensively throughout Mexico. One objective of his writing is to share the nuances of Mexican culture unknown to most. In addition to teaching, traveling, and writing, he spends time in the gym, attempting to stay fit. He also enjoys cooking and relaxing with his partner of nine years, Francisco Orrantia. He won the 2010 Lambda Literary Award in the gay romance category.

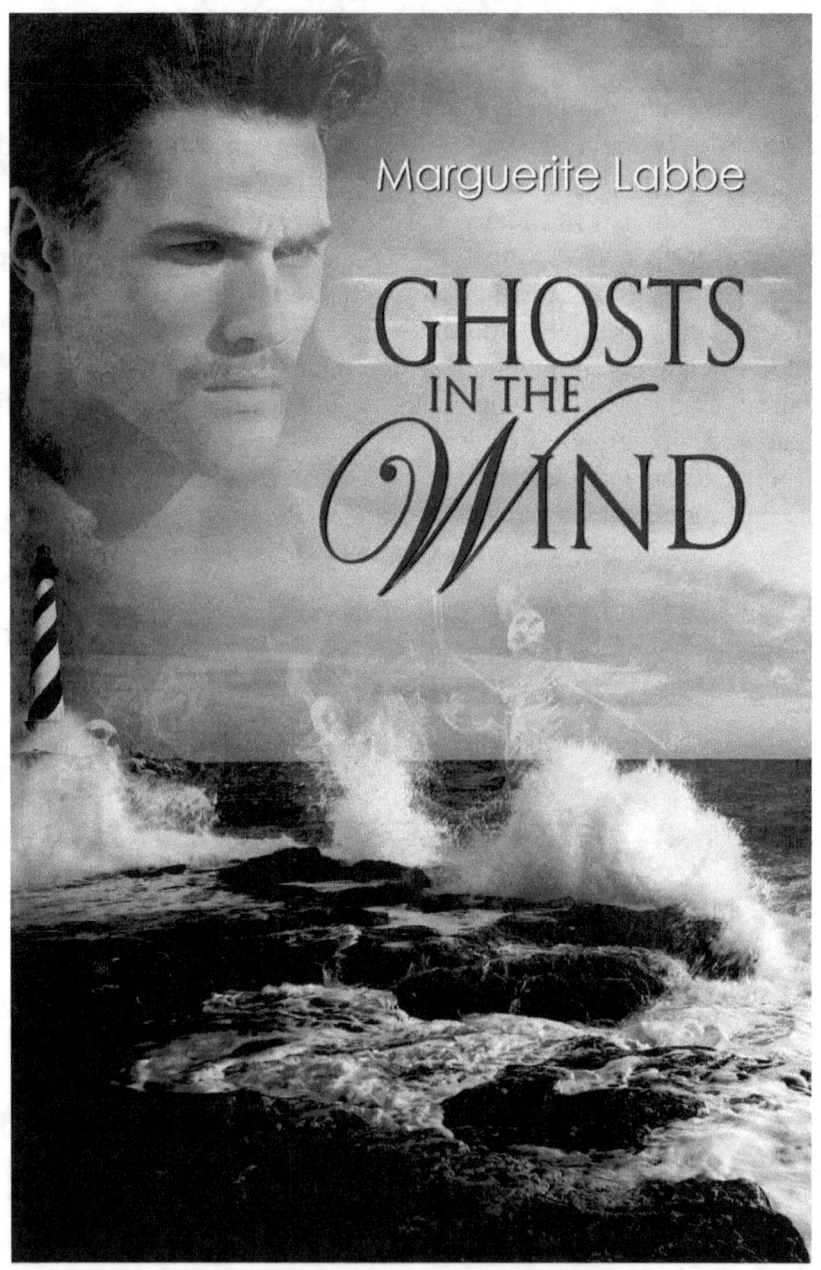

www.ingramcontent.com/pod-product-compliance
Lightning Source LLC
Chambersburg PA
CBHW070125260626
47160CB00004B/1622